An Inconvenient

Companion

Audrey Harrison

An Inconvenient Companion

by

Audrey Harrison

Published by Audrey Harrison

Copyright 2014 Audrey Harrison

This book was proof read by Rob Van De Laak, a man with patience and who offers advice with humour, a couple of grumbles and a lot of sense! He can be contacted on http://robvandelaak.blogspot.com/

Dedication

This book is dedicated to my mum, Margaret Horrobin.

My mum always wanted me to write a book about the servants, so here you are mum, a book for you! Although your namesake does actually appear in An Inconvenient Wife, this is the book that the staff have their own stories.

Hope you enjoy it.

Lots of love, Audrey.

Prologue

London, spring 1816

Alfred Peters, one of the new Bow Street Officers visited Baron Kersal's home in London for the third time that week. His colleague, Martin Corless, was following the Baron in his day to day life, but it had been Alfred's role to infiltrate the inner circle. Lord Halkyn, an aristocrat who disliked the way Baron Kersal was developing his business, had provided the means to access the house and Alfred had worked in his usual methodical way, liaising with Corless until they had gathered enough evidence against Baron Kersal.

The Baron, in addition to running a house seven miles outside the city, where a variety of pursuits that were not discussed in polite circles were held, had decided that he needed more funds and had branched out further. He had begun arranging the kidnap and forced marriages of innocent young girls, which was when Lord Halkyn had become involved. One usually used to enjoying some of the pleasures that Baron Kersal offered, he had helped to rescue Miss Charlotte Webster, who had been kidnapped. Once Miss Webster had been safe Lord Halkyn had vowed, with the assistance of Bow Street, to bring the Baron to justice.

Alfred had been introduced as Lord Halkyn's cousin and had convinced the Baron and his friends that he was a keen gambler. He had secured a lot of information through one of the girls, Laura, who had helped Charlotte. Laura had disliked the new activity, particularly as the girls being targeted were young. Alfred, being the man that he was, had given the informant enough money to ensure that when the time came Laura would be able to get herself out of danger.

Everything was coming together as they had hoped. He had not needed to visit the premises again really, but something had drawn him to it, one last time. Alfred had always acted professionally, he took his job very seriously, but Laura had haunted his dreams since the evening he had met her. She had seemed a kindred spirit, older than her years, a little like himself, having seen more of life than any decent human being should

5

have. He had told her that they would never see each other again and although he had visited the premises numerous times, he had always stayed away from the girls that were available.

This night though, he could not concentrate. He knew exactly why he had visited the house and the fight with his conscience only meant that he did not focus fully on gambling and was running at a loss. He tossed his cards onto the table and with a sigh, pushed his chair back; his lack of success was giving the Baron back some of the money that he had won earlier in the week.

Baron Kersal approached the young man, always ready to persuade a gambler to try and win back his losses, usually resulting in further losses for the player and more profit for himself.

"Good evening Mr Peters," the Baron said genially. "Giving up so easily?"

"Yes, I'm not in the mood tonight," Alfred responded, taking a pinch of snuff.

"Some other entertainment then?" the Baron offered, always ready to offer something that would cost his visitors.

Albert paused; this was the moment that he should walk out of the door and never look back. He took another pinch of snuff while fighting with his demons. He snapped his snuffbox shut and placed it carefully in his pocket.

"If that girl is available who I saw on my first visit, I think I could be tempted," he said with a convincing leer.

"Who was that?" the Baron asked, pleased that he would be receiving further money from the young man.

"Laura, she was worth the money my cousin and I paid, she was very obliging, no matter what we did," Albert said, trying not to look too keen about seeing Laura again.

The Baron frowned. "Laura does other jobs for me these days, what about one of our other girls? Some of the younger ones are more than willing to spend an evening with a handsome young man."

Alfred, with his tall slim frame, dark hair and green eyes, set in a pale complexion, could be described as ordinary, but never handsome. Anyone taking the time to look into his eyes would see a haunted expression, the result of seeing hardship and facing danger too many times. Alfred struggled to maintain his pleasant expression; he really disliked the Baron and would be happy when his colleagues raided the establishment.

"Laura had specialities that I enjoyed. I would be willing to pay extra for her, but if not...." he left the sentence hanging, sure of the Baron's reaction to money.

Not one to disappoint, the Baron replied immediately, "Laura will be with you in ten minutes. If you would like to follow me, we can agree a price."

Alfred nodded and followed the portly, glistening man into his office, where he conducted most transactions. It was better to be away from the eyes of the other visitors, especially when dealing with men who had lost a fortune gambling. He may not look as if he was anything other than an overweight aristocrat with questionable tastes, but Alfred knew that his type could prove to be the most dangerous. If they could not protect themselves physically, men like the Baron always made sure that they surrounded themselves with loyal staff who could.

When the deal had been done, a member of staff took him to a bedroom.

As with the Baron's other bedrooms, the room was minimally furnished, excess furniture was a waste of money in the Baron's eyes. The décor was clean and tidy, which was a higher standard than some of the other places that existed for the same reasons, but it was not extravagant. Everything in the house was there for the purpose of separating money from the visitors who visited there. The door was left open while there was no girl in attendance. Alfred poured himself a glass of wine,

7

beginning to realise what he was about to do. He drank the wine back in one gulp and poured himself another.

"Does an evening with me cause you to turn to drink?" came a voice from the doorway.

Alfred turned to see Laura, leaning against the doorway, a smile on her face. Alfred smiled in return and indicated that she should come into the room, by offering her a glass of wine. "Hello Laura," he said quietly.

He watched her as she walked into the room, closing the door behind her and letting her shawl fall over the chair, before accepting the glass of wine. She was not stunningly beautiful, but her auburn hair and dark green eyes drew him to her like a moth to a flame. She had signs of wrinkles developing, a mark of the difficulties in her life, she must only be aged around four and twenty. Girls in her trade started young and were cast off before they got too old. Like him, Laura had aged prematurely, a consequence of the struggle of being born on the wrong side of polite society.

"You've been a regular visitor here recently, I was disappointed when our first encounter didn't tempt you back," she flirted, as she sipped her wine, looking at him over the edge of the glass.

"I'm here now," Alfred said, his face never changing expression, but his insides feeling lighter at the fact that she had shown an interest in him by knowing that he had been on the premises. No one else would have taken notice, he was not handsome enough or rich enough, to be noticed by the girls who worked there.

"Yes, you are," Laura said circling him, provocatively. "And what do you have in mind for tonight? Is it going to be different to last time?"

She was asking him if he was going to talk to her, which was all they had done on that first meeting, well, except for the two kisses they had shared. "I always think different is best, don't you?" he responded.

Laura flushed slightly, but maintained the banter. There were peep holes in every room, so they could be being watched. Neither of them could give anything away, or they would not get out of house in one piece. "I am here to please you, sir."

"You can start by getting undressed," Alfred said, refilling his glass. He should get her on the bed behind the covers, so that she would not be seen by anyone choosing to watch the activities of the house, rather than take part. He wanted to see her undress though and he knew that the eyes watching would not be too interested at this point, they preferred the activity further on.

"As you wish," Laura responded. She slowly undressed herself. All her clothing was made to enable it to be removed easily, too many fastenings could result in ripped clothing and that cost money to repair. She had no corset on, again for ease, and was soon stood naked before Alfred.

"What about you, sir?" she asked, trying to keep the anticipation and warmth from her voice. As much as she had haunted Alfred's dreams, he had haunted hers.

"All in good time," Alfred said, placing his glass on the small table and striding towards her. He grabbed her and kissed her as he had kissed her last time, as if it would be his last. Laura responded to him immediately, wrapping her arms about his neck and pulling him further into her.

Alfred did not stop kissing her as he lifted her from her feet and carried her over to the bed. He climbed on after her and closed the curtains around them. There would be nothing more for the peeping toms to look at that night.

*

Hours later, Laura was nestled in Alfred's arms, facing his chest. She had never nestled with any other client, it was always do what had to be done and then once finished, more than likely on to the next client. She forced her thoughts not to dwell on her job and snuggled further into the warmth surrounding her.

"What are you doing woman?" Alfred chuckled, but he kept his voice low, not risking any conversation being heard by anyone else.

"You said I would never see you again," Laura said quietly.

"I tried to stay away," Alfred said. "I'm putting you at risk being here."

"It's a risk I'm willing to take," Laura said, kissing the smattering of hair that curled on his chest.

Alfred paused from stroking her back, "Laura, I cannot offer you anything," he said. She would not have a happy time being linked to him.

"I have not asked for anything have I?" Laura replied, still quietly, but the indignation was clear in her voice.

"Sorry, I just don't want you to get hurt," Alfred replied, kissing her, until she smiled.

"I don't want you to get hurt either," Laura responded eventually, but not pulling away fully from his lips. He had hinted previously that Bow Street Officers did not have a long life span and she had worried that he would come to harm.

"I know, you told me that when we first met," Alfred said, remembering the words that she had said to him.

"In another life I would have taken care of you," Laura whispered the words, as if reading his thoughts.

"In another life I would have let you," Alfred responded as he had on that first day.

No other words were exchanged as they showed each other through actions how much the words meant to them both.

Deep in the night, Alfred finally stirred. "It is time I left; if I stay any longer questions will be asked."

"I know, I was just being selfish," Laura said, a lump developing in her insides that she knew by instinct would be hard to move. This time he would not return, she knew that without any words being said.

"Kersal said that you didn't usually do this sort of thing anymore. He isn't mistreating you is he?" Alfred asked. Case or no case, if she was being hurt, he would sort the Baron out himself.

"No he isn't," Laura said. "I'm looking after the girls here; apparently I'm getting too old to see the gentlemen."

"How old are you, you old hag?" Alfred asked teasingly.

"Four and twenty, does that shock you?" Laura responded with mock primness.

"As a man who is a whole year younger, no it doesn't shock me, although I may have to try a younger model in future, just to see the difference," Alfred said, before having the wind knocked out of him by Laura poking him in his ribs. "Oooff woman, you are vicious!" he laughed, still careful to keep his voice low.

Alfred became serious and held Laura tightly to him. "I do have to leave now, but promise me that you will be careful," he said.

"I will," Laura said, blinking back tears that had threatened to spring to her eyes at such concern. She mentally shook herself, there was no place for tears in her world, life was what it was. There was no point repining now. She climbed out of bed and quickly got dressed.

Alfred followed her from the bed and dressed himself. He approached Laura and gave her a hand full of coins. "Thank you Laura," he said, kissing her roughly on her lips before walking out of the room without looking back.

Laura stayed still a few moments before leaving the room and returning to her own private bed chamber. Once there she sat on the edge of the bed and wrapped her arms around her middle. "God, if you exist and you are fair, you will let me keep this little part of him. The future is too bleak with no reminder of him in it."

Chapter 1

Somerset, autumn 1816

"That blasted man!" Martha Fairfield, housekeeper and former companion to Lady Elizabeth Dunham muttered to herself as she walked through the hall of Dunham House. She was always so calm, so collected, except when she was faced with Mr Charles Anderton and his interfering ways.

Why could he not keep to his own role of Lord Dunham's man of business? She grumbled to herself as she stomped up the stairs. Martha Fairfield never stomped and it proved just how annoyed she was that she threw caution to the wind and allowed the footmen to see how agitated she was.

He was always *there*, offering his so-called help, giving his unwanted advice on matters that should not, no, did not concern him. Whoever heard of a man of business helping to find a nanny? There were clear lines of responsibility in every household and Charles Anderton consistently crossed them. Well, he did when it had anything to do with her responsibilities, he never seemed to interfere with the butler or the cook, the way he did with her role. His actions resulted in Martha coming to the conclusion that he had no faith in her abilities, something that she was reminded of time and time again.

Initially, when they had first met, she had presumed that it was because he saw her as a Lady's companion and to be fair, many in that role had little wit about them. She had come across women who held the role, who had virtually no education or conversation that showed any level of intelligence or understanding. Being grouped with them, although a tad unfair, was not really a surprise and she had not felt any great antagonism, although he had managed to irritate her regularly.

Now though, Charles Anderton had known her for well over a year, and in that time there had been a lot of contact between the pair. At one time they were on an equal footing, desperate that their master and mistress would overcome the hurdles they had faced and acknowledge the attraction that existed between them. It had given Martha and Charles a common cause that they had both tried to work on in the background in helping their employers along the way.

That felt a long time ago now though, Martha reflected as she closed the door on her bed chamber for a moment. She did not usually escape from her duties during the day, but something Charles had said, had hit a nerve and she needed to gather her thoughts before continuing on with her tasks.

All he had said was that she had no experience with children and nannies, which was true, but she had taken it as a personal insult. For some reason his words had made her feel less of a woman, somewhat irrationally, she acknowledged to herself. She struggled with the feelings coursing through her body, as the implication of the words had stirred something deep within her. It was something that she usually managed to suppress.

She sighed and sat at her window seat, picking up a cushion and holding it tight against her stomach. She tried to calm herself, looking out of the Jacobean building and over the garden. The view was of the garden that spread out on the side of the property. It was a beautiful view that she enjoyed being able to see each day, and she had enjoyed watching the changes in the seasons, since the gardeners at Dunham House excelled themselves. Her shoulders slumped. She knew what her destiny was; and had accepted it a long time ago. Why did Charles Anderton have to stir feelings that would haunt her long into the night?

*

Martha Fairfield had been born into a genteel family. There were no titles linked to the family name, but there was enough wealth to provide a comfortable lifestyle. Martha was the eldest girl in a family of five children. Her two older brothers had indulged their baby sister, even when a younger brother and sister had been born. It was a happy, but uneventful life.

Martha was brought up to expect to marry a gentleman, probably someone that was known to the family already. She would continue to live in the area of Cheshire that she had been born to, bringing up her own family in familiar surroundings, with friends and family. Only she was to find out that life sometimes did not always follow what was expected of it.

Her father died suddenly of a seizure. He was still young and it was a complete shock to everyone who knew him. That, for the Fairfield family was not to be the only shock they had to endure. Their father had not been as good with his finances as they had presumed. They had been living in blissful ignorance until his death was announced officially, and the creditors called in what was owed to them.

Martha's older brother Thomas had acted quickly and had sold off some of the land to pay off the debt, he was a proud young man and refused to leave the debts outstanding. The continued good name of the family was important to all of them, moreso with the new financial difficulties. Thomas then had the difficult task of sitting his family down and explaining the consequence of paying off the creditors. It was a difficult conversation in which he told them that their property would no longer sustain the family.

Martha's mother had taken the news badly, partly still grieving for her husband and partly through shame of what had gone on without her knowledge. Her children had tried to reassure her, but she had taken to her bed for the foreseeable future, giving Thomas the further difficulty of dealing with an invalid mother and the costs associated with that.

The second eldest, William had immediately informed the family that he was signing up to join the navy. He had always wanted to, but had been persuaded into following a career in the clergy. The potential of joining the navy and earning more money while following the career he wanted, was too much of a pull. At the same time as having the career he had longed for, he would have the ability to send some money to his family each month, so it was a decision he found easy to make.

The youngest boy was too young to work, so would stay within the family home. Thomas decided that he would look to have him apprenticed when he was old enough.

Martha realised through the conversations which were held, that she herself, and her younger sister Susan, would have to secure a marriage and soon. Susan was too young, but she would need to be married almost as soon as she left the schoolroom, something which was not ideal in anyone's mind. In her own case, Martha had come out the previous year and although had not received an offer of marriage yet, there were one or two young men that she thought may offer for her in time. Thomas spoke to his sister about her situation in private.

"I didn't want to have this conversation in front of the others," he explained as they sat together in what had been his father's study.

"What is it?" Martha asked gently, thinking that her brother had aged over the last few months and she felt sorry for what he had faced and the decisions he had had to make.

"Is there anyone who wishes to marry you now Martha?" he asked gently.

"No, but I have only had one season, I don't consider myself on the shelf just yet," Martha teased.

"Neither do I," Thomas smiled at his sister, but the smile was tinged with sadness. "The problem is Martha, we cannot afford another season for you."

Martha looked at her brother, and the serious expression on his face helped the words to sink in. By not being able to afford another season, she would not be out socialising, which meant that she would not come into contact with any gentlemen. That lack of social interaction would guarantee that there would be no marriage proposals forthcoming. There were enough young ladies looking to marry for the available gentlemen not to have to search for someone they had met the previous year. Especially if she would no longer be attending the parties and therefore out of their social circle. Thomas was effectively telling Martha that he could not help her to marry, condemning her to spinsterhood.

"Susan?" Martha asked quietly.

"Not even a first season unless things change dramatically in the next four years," Thomas said sadly. "I'm sorry Martha, I would if I could, but even without the expense of a season, the land we have left isn't going to sustain us. I'm letting most of the staff go, William going the navy will help, one less mouth to feed and I think I will be able to get Henry apprenticed next year, but I cannot afford the expense which the rounds of entertainments would cost."

"Of course you can't," Martha said practically. She suppressed the feelings of sadness and bitterness at what she had lost. It was not Thomas's fault, he was doing the best he could in the circumstances. She could spend her time hating her father, but all that would achieve would be to embitter herself, since her feelings towards him could not affect him. She had to be practical and help her family. "If things are so bad I need to help as well."

"You will need to take on some extra duties around the house, without staff there will be more work for us all to do," Thomas said.

"Thomas, I cannot be a burden on you for the rest of my days," Martha said with a firm set to her mouth. "A spinster sister is a drain on what are already limited resources, and you cannot have such a burden for the remainder of my life. I will seek a position as a Lady's companion, I have not the ability to be a governess, but I can be a companion."

"No!" Thomas said. "The situation is not that bad!"

Martha reached over and squeezed her brother's hand. "You need help, so let me do as William is doing, and send some of my money home. It won't be much, but you will have no expense from me and I can feel that I am helping. Maybe by the time Susan comes of age, things will be a little different."

"I am condemning you to a life of drudgery," Thomas said quietly, taking hold of his sister's hands.

"You are not!" Martha exclaimed. "We could all end in debtor's prison if we do not pull together as a family. I am happy to do this Thomas, it is for the best."

Martha had pushed aside her feelings of what could have been and secured a position with a lady who lived twenty miles away from Martha's home. It meant that Martha could travel home twice a year and see her family. The lady was old, but not an unkind mistress and Martha genuinely cared for her. Martha felt real sadness when three years later the lady died and Martha lost her position.

She returned home temporarily. Her employer had left her a hundred pounds in her will, an unexpected windfall for Martha. She gave Thomas half the money and kept half for herself. She was practical enough to realise that at some point she would need some money for her retirement and although she could save little out of her wages, with sending money back home, a legacy such as this could not be squandered.

When looking for another position, Martha decided to look for a younger person. She had enjoyed her time with her employer, but she did not want to be constantly grieving over the loss of people who came to mean something to her. She had mourned her dead employer as much as she would have done if she had been a family member.

Thomas had by chance heard of a man in Lancashire looking for a companion for his young daughter. Martha visited the property and met the young Elizabeth Rufford and accepted the offer of an appointment.

When, ten years later Elizabeth had married her guardian, Lord Dunham, Martha had resigned herself to the fact that she would have to seek another post, but Elizabeth would hear none of it. The pair were more than employer and employee, more like a mixture of sister, companion and mother all rolled into one. Elizabeth had insisted that Martha had to stay with her, and when an opening arose in Lord Dunham's household, Martha became the new Housekeeper. She had not wanted to take up Elizabeth's offer of being with her without a defined role.

Martha was happy, in the main. She was sending money home regularly. Her promotion from companion to housekeeper meant that she was able to continue to build a nest egg for herself, adding to the money she had already saved. She was content in her role, except where Charles Anderton was involved. He was Lord Dunham's man of business and very efficient, but every time he tried to 'help'........Martha could not bear his interference.

His regular offers of assistance had the effect of making her feel insecure in her position. He had never undermined her as such; it was just his manner that seemed to imply that he doubted her abilities. There was just the one time that he had been there when she needed him, Martha shook herself, but she would not let herself dwell on that incident. She had shown her vulnerability then, and it was not an event she wanted to dwell on for a number of reasons.

She stood and wiped her hands across her face. Not one for dwelling on things that were out of her control, she pulled herself together once more. It was time to learn not to take everything he said to heart, they would be working together for a long time to come. An image of another life flashed before her eyes too quickly for her to suppress it. She felt an ache in her heart, before she pushed it away. She grumbled to herself about her stupidity and strode towards her bedroom door. There was work to be done, and she could afford no more of this maudlin mood.

Chapter 2

Charles Anderton gave Martha a wide berth for the following few days after their latest altercation. He could not avoid her completely, the house was large, but their employers very often invited Charles and Martha to share their meals with them. It was quite unusual for this to happen in an aristocrat's house, but both Lord and Lady Dunham would never be described as your usual aristocrat.

He puzzled over Martha's reaction to his offer of help. He thought they were over the bickering and one-upmanship that had occurred when they first met. It had been a childish ploy on his part he admitted to himself. He had met the pretty, prim Miss Fairfield and had for some unknown reason wanted to ruffle her. He had set about it in his own way. He could not be openly teasing, because that would be frowned upon, but he soon realised that when he seemed to be offering his assistance, she could not control her responses.

He thought she was delightful when annoyed, as her usually pale complexion heightened in colour and her blue eyes flashed deep marine blue. Charles had never wanted to make her feel uncomfortable, in fact he had been attracted to her from the start, but she had always seemed so controlled, so composed, that he had wanted to see if there was any way he could bring some discomfort to her composure.

Charles knew that he should have behaved better when they had first met. The situation had quickly gone further than Charles had anticipated, and he cursed himself time and time again when yet another set of terse words had been exchanged. His initial behaviour had resulted in a dislike of him on her part. He very often wondered at his stupidity, he liked her but all he had achieved was to ensure she disliked him with a passion.

It was his own fault, he cursed to himself on a regular basis. If he had not been influenced by his own insecurity he probably would have a very good relationship with Miss Fairfield by now. Unfortunately, he was now convinced that would never happen.

The problem, he acknowledged only to himself, was that she made him feel inferior. She did nothing intentionally, and he was convinced that there was no malicious streak to be found anywhere in Martha Fairfield, but when he had first met her she had seemed so much above him in rank, he had acted in a way to try to shake her position. He had never wanted her to get into trouble with their employers, but it was his blundering way of trying to make sure that he felt more secure in his own position.

He felt ashamed sometimes of the foolish things he had done and said to get a reaction out of Martha. She had reacted to him, he smiled to himself, there was fire under that calm exterior, but the result had not been to make him feel secure, but to create a real dislike of him on her part.

He mulled over why he still felt insecure after the years in his post with Lord Dunham. His start in life had been humble, he had been working in the school that Lord Dunham attended, as a runner for the students. An unlikely bond had developed between the pair, probably because of Charles' inability to keep his thoughts to himself about some of the students that attended the school. Lord Dunham, then plain Michael Birchall, had found Charles' mutterings funny and their friendship had developed.

After two years, the then Lord Dunham had been approached by his heir and been persuaded to offer Charles a place as an apprentice for his uncle's man of business. Charles had been astonished that anyone would offer him such an opportunity and was overwhelmed at his feeling of obligation to the young man who had spoken up for him. He had perhaps not recognised that Michael had seen the frustration that Charles tried to suppress about the menial tasks he had to perform, with little hope of promotion, or that he had seen the intelligence that was always on show.

Charles had taken the position and over the next few years had worked harder than he had ever done, but this time it was work that he throve on. He learned as much as he possibly could, watching, listening, helping and never tiring. It would have been heaven apart from the behaviour of some of the staff who worked in the household. Charles would never have imagined that there was a hierarchy within an aristocrat's house, but there was. Some of the staff objected to an unknown young boy being added to the household, when there were others who thought they should have had the opportunity.

The disgruntled few made sure that at every opportunity Charles was fully aware that he was not worthy of the role he held. It was only by knowing the nephew that he had gained his position, not because of his own abilities. Although Charles tried to ignore the jibes, when said enough times it was almost inevitable that they would be believed.

When the opportunity arose to be the man of business for Michael Birchall, who was still at that time, the heir to the then Lord Dunham, Charles grasped the opportunity. He would be managing a single gentleman's business, not the huge household, which was the Dunham estate.

By working with Michael, Charles' confidence had increased. His employer always considered his opinions and treated him almost as an equal. Charles flourished and became even more competent. The sudden death of Lord Dunham thrust both Michael and Charles into roles they had not been expecting. Michael became the new Lord Dunham, and Charles became the man of business for a Lord of the realm, back in the household that had undermined him as a young man.

Returning to the house, with the full support of the Lord, meant that the staff who still worked there treated Charles differently. This time he was not a young boy learning the ropes, but a man confident in his abilities and prepared to stand up to anyone that doubted him. There was no hint of the comments that had been made previously, but Charles still felt insecure. He sometimes felt that he had been promoted above his station in life, and meeting a woman like Martha Fairfield only added to that insecurity.

She was confident and competent. A gentleman's daughter, who really should have been part of the family, rather than working for it. The first time they had met, Charles had been struck by her appearance, she was not stunningly beautiful, but handsome, and with her air of composure and dignity, Charles had thought her very attractive. So, he should have welcomed her, cultivated their friendship in the hope that it would develop and then be happy with his lot. Instead, he had allowed his insecurity about not being good enough to surface and had antagonised her at every opportunity, until it had become almost second nature.

Recently, he had started to try and help her, in an effort to make amends for their poor beginning. He would not normally have bothered, not being one to pursue something that was hopeless, but there had been a glimmer of hope. When Lady Dunham had been in danger, Miss Fairfield had turned to him for help. She had been so shaken as to break down in tears. He had assured her that he would bring Lady Dunham back and he had asked Martha to trust him. She had replied that she did, it had nearly rocked him backwards with surprise, but he had managed to remain focused on the matter in hand.

Only later had he allowed himself to dwell on her words. If she believed and trusted him, surely she could not dislike him to the level she appeared to? He decided that there was hope for him after all and he was determined to help her whenever he could. He was doing it to spend more time with her and to hopefully convince her that he was not the demon she had thought he was.

His long term aim was unclear. Relations between staff were frowned upon in any household, so he had convinced himself that he would work hard until she liked him and then at least they could enjoy working together. It was obvious that neither would ever leave their employer until their age forced them to. A good employer was always worth keeping hold of, but the feelings went further with Charles and Martha. They cared for their employers as if they were family, they were their family in many respects.

He had thought that by offering to help to find a nanny it would relieve some pressure from Martha's workload. Lady Dunham's baby had arrived earlier than everyone had expected, so a nanny had not yet been appointed. With the need for extra organisation which a new baby brought, Martha's work had increased. They had employed a nurse for the child's early months, but a nanny was needed to take over the role of carer for the little girl.

As soon as he had offered his help, he had seen her face change as she struggled to maintain her composure, and he immediately knew that he had erred. Charles had tried to explain that he had wanted to help ease her workload, but it had not seemed to ease the anger his words had caused.

"I am fully aware of your lack of confidence in my abilities, there is no reason for you to explain your motivation," Miss Fairfield had responded angrily. The stiffening of her body and flushing of her cheeks were a clear outward sign of the struggle going on within to maintain her usual calm.

"It has nothing to do with your ability as housekeeper, I just thought that with you having no experience of children, or nannies, that I may be able to offer some advice...," Charles replied, trying desperately to retrieve the situation.

"And you have obviously had so much more experience than I," came the sarcastic response. "I have no real experience of clearing out fire grates, but I am perfectly capable of appointing a house maid to do the task. I shall employ the nanny to Lady Dunham's requirements without anyone else's interference! Perhaps if you confined your thoughts to your own position, it would make life a lot happier for us all," came the prim response. "Please excuse me, I have things to do, for which, no, I do not require your help."

She had left the room, almost slamming the door behind her, and Charles had been left to curse his lack of progress with the woman. He did not know what to do to make her see that he liked her, it was obvious that he had more ground to make up than he had first thought.

Three days after the incident with Miss Fairfield, Charles was offered the break from her company that he thought might do him good. He was becoming too focused on how he could make her see that he was not the person to be angry at all the time.

Lord Dunham had spoken to him after going through his morning post. "Charles, I have a journey I need you to make."

"Yes my Lord?" Charles asked, putting down his pen and turning to face Lord Dunham. Both men worked together in Lord Dunham's study during the morning. It was the time when they needed to be in each other's company. Once their work was done, Charles would retire to a small office at the rear of the house, or be out on the land, while Lord Dunham usually spent some time outdoors with his wife.

The couple enjoyed the open air, and come rain or shine, could be seen striding or riding out over the fields before coming home for the evening. Lady Dunham had worked on the estate prior to the birth of her child, and although recently she had taken a less active role in actually carrying out the work, she still took a great interest in what was happening.

"I've received a letter from Lady Dunham's property, Home Farm," Lord Dunham started, indicating a letter on his desk. "Mr Lawson writes to say that he has not been in good health recently and although the work he is undertaking is light in comparison with other estate managers, he does not feel he is able to carry it on for much longer. He does not wish for the estate to fall into disrepair because of him."

"Ah, I see," Charles replied. Lady Dunham had purchased the estate in Yorkshire before marrying Lord Dunham. She had thought it was the place that she would spend the rest of her life, not being the typical woman that society wanted. Lord Dunham had fallen in love with her, but as her guardian had not acted on his feelings for a long time and had worked with his ward to secure the property.

Charles had been involved with the purchase of the estate in Yorkshire and the appointment of Mr Lawson. The elderly man had been cast off by Lady Dunham's cousin, Herbert Rufford, when he had taken over Lady Dunham's father's estate. There had been a dispute between the cousins,

25

in which Lady Dunham had been sent to her guardian. At that time no one was aware as to what lengths Herbert and his wife would go to in trying to obtain Lady Dunham's pre-marriage fortune.

Lord Dunham had suggested that Mr Lawson work on the Yorkshire estate, as it was relatively small and he could enjoy a form of semi-retirement. It appeared now though, that even that was too much for the elderly man.

"If you go to Home Farm, you can spend some time there, making sure Mr Lawson is settled into the cottage he was promised and appoint a new manager at the same time," Lord Dunham explained. "Elizabeth will need to be reassured that you have appointed someone capable, or she will be travelling across the country herself," he finished with a smile.

"I will do my utmost," Charles assured his master. "How soon do you want me to leave?"

"I need to go to London in a few days," Lord Dunham said. "Please send a return letter to Mr Lawson, explaining that we accept what he is saying and that you will be with him in ten days."

"I shall do it immediately, my Lord," Charles responded, turning back to his work.

A break away from Dunham House would be worthwhile, especially if it made a certain housekeeper miss his company Charles thought, as he penned a letter.

Chapter 3

London, autumn 1816

Laura knew she was being followed, the man had been keeping track of her since she had left the warehouse at the side of the Thames. It was not a place she would ever want to return to, but if she did not get away from her pursuer, it was highly likely that she would meet the same fate that Clara had.

Laura had shared a room with Clara since Baron Kersal's house of ill repute had been forced to close down. They had stuck together, trying to stay away from that kind of work again. For Laura, there was no chance of being a lady of the night in her current state, but she did not want to return to that line of work in the future either.

They had each made plans, both wanting to escape the grime of the London that they belonged to. Laura had money put aside, but Clara had delayed because she had thought one of her regular customers would offer her support. The foolish girl, Laura muttered to herself. She had not realised that she was nothing but a piece of meat to the men that had visited the house, to be used and thrown away. Just because one man asked for you each time he visited, it did not mean he held you in any affection.

Clara's regular customer had not killed her, Laura was sure of that. Those type of men tended not to add murder to their bad habits, and she was convinced this had more to do with Baron Kersal. The Baron had extended his services into kidnapping and forced marriages and it was that extension into illegal activity that had brought his business to an end. Unfortunately for all who were involved, instead of hanging as he should have done, he had been supported by a Duke and the trial had collapsed.

Laura had thought, naively, that that would be the end of it, but it seemed not. Clara had come home one day to say that Sarah had disappeared. Sarah, was one of the girls who knew about the forced marriages. There had only been a small circle who had been involved.

Clara was not worried about Sarah's disappearance until Laura found out that another girl who knew about the activity, Veronica, had also mysteriously 'gone to visit relatives'.

Laura knew for a fact that Veronica did not have any relatives and immediately was on the alert. Something was not right. She tried to persuade Clara to leave immediately, they could have got on the stage that very day, but Clara had asked for one more day. She was desperate to contact her gentleman friend, sure that if he knew her situation he would help.

One of the errand boys from the local hostelry had come banging on Laura's door two days later, saying that Miss Clara had been found. Laura had followed him to the warehouse where her body was. She had been thrown in the Thames, whether dead or alive, Laura had no idea, but Clara's body was an image that would remain with Laura for the rest of her life. For how long that was going to be, Laura was not sure as she hurried through the streets with the errand boy.

She had noticed the man watching her as she identified Clara's body and watched it being taken away. Clara would have a pauper's burial. It was only that Laura and Clara lived so close to the water's edge that Laura had even found out that Clara was discovered. A body in the Thames was more commonly left unidentified.

The warehouse area was busy, so seeing a man there was nothing out of the ordinary, in fact seeing a body being dragged out of the water always had the effect of a small crowd gathering. Laura had noticed the man because of the fact that he did not want to be noticed and had hung back in the shadows.

Although upset at seeing her friend's lifeless and slightly swollen body, Laura had enough survival instincts to be practical. She feigned the vapours and persuaded the errand boy to take her away from the area. If she had company, she might have a little protection, but not much. They walked quickly and Laura said quietly that she needed to visit a church.

They approached St Andrew's church and Laura gave the boy a coin and sent him on his way. She entered the church and sat down in the front pew. The more on view she was, the safer she was. She knelt to pray, all the time surreptitiously watching the rear of the church. Her pursuer had followed her into the building and sat at the rear of the church.

For a long time, Laura sat in the pew, rather than kneeling as if in prayer, but she had no intention of moving. The building was not crowded, but there were people coming and going, enough to offer her some protection. She needed to seek help, but had to wait for the right moment. If she moved too early, her efforts to stay safe could be in vain.

Two hours passed before the clergyman approached her. He was an older man, with greying hair and his clothing was slightly worn. There was no expensive living for him in this part of London. He sat by her side and said gently, "You have been here a long time, my child."

"Yes, I am in trouble and have nowhere else to go. At least I am safe here, please don't send me away," Laura said quietly.

"I could never send someone away who seeks safety in the Lord's house," he responded kindly. "Can we help you? I can assure you that pews are not the most comfortable thing to sleep on, if you intend to stay indefinitely."

Laura smiled slightly, but then paused before speaking. "You would not believe me if I told you," she replied. She did not want to end up in Bedlam accused of being a lunatic.

"In my time I have seen and heard things I would not wish anyone to hear," came the reassuring response. "All I want to do is help, but without knowing what you are facing, I am working on supposition."

Laura sighed, accepting the reality, which was that this was the best chance she had. Not accustomed to trusting anyone, it was a huge step for her. "There is a man sat at the back of this church who is here to do me harm. The people I have worked with," she flushed at the thought of speaking about such a profession in a church. "Have disappeared one by one, and I am convinced that he is here to inflict the same fate on me."

The clergyman did not react or turn around. "Are you sure about this?" he asked calmly, his voice giving nothing away.

"I have just come from seeing my friend's body which was dragged from the river, another two friends have disappeared, with one supposedly going to family that don't exist. I can only think they have received the same fate as Clara," Laura said worriedly.

"Why would anyone want to see you disappear?"

"We know about illegal activity," Laura whispered. "There was going to be a trial, but one of the top nobs spoke up for the man involved and he got off. I can only think that he is making sure nothing can happen to threaten his safety in the future. Our lives our cheap, no one will notice when we disappear," Laura said with a shudder. "That is what I am trying to escape from, but I understand if you don't believe me, I could be a madwoman off the streets."

"I have no reason to mistrust what you say," the clergyman reassured her. He was fully aware of how cheap life was in these parts. He sat for a few moments before speaking again. "Will the father of your child not help?"

Laura flushed a deep red, she had hoped that her swelling stomach had not been noticed. "I need to reach him," she replied honestly. "He does not know about the child, but he is my only chance of reaching safety."

The clergyman presumed that the father was some kind of gentleman and doubted that the young woman sitting before him would receive any sort of help from such a man, but he was not about to turn his back on her. The story she had told could be lies, but he had believed her. There were no embellishments and he read the newspapers, and did remember something about a trial involving a member of the aristocracy collapsing.

"I have a suggestion that I think may work," he said eventually. "You have a distinctive red cloak and your hair colouring is similar to my girl of all works. If we can get you into the vestry you can change places with Beth and she can return and sit in the pew for a time. I can't promise to keep her here all day, I don't want to put her in any danger, but I can give you enough time to get away."

"Thank you," Laura breathed. Her shoulders sagging in relief.

"Make sure you turn and face the back of the church fully as we make our way into the vestry," the clergyman instructed.

"Why?" Laura asked, alarmed.

"I want it easily proven when Beth takes your cloak off that she is not you. Facially you are totally different and I want that made clear, to our unwelcome visitor. I don't want Beth coming to any harm," the clergyman explained.

"I understand and will make sure he has a clear view of my face," Laura agreed. She may be afraid, but she would never put someone else at risk in her efforts to reach safety.

The clergyman stood and said in a clear voice, "You may follow me, but all I can offer is some water. I cannot be expected to feed you when you are not a regular parishioner." His tone was stern, but his expression did not mirror the sound of his voice and he led the way out of the pew and towards the vestry.

Laura moved to the end of the pew and looked to the back of the church. The man that had followed her was staring at her intently, obviously working out whether or not to follow her. He looked away when she caught his eye. Laura continued into the vestry, content that her face had been clear.

Beth was already being spoken to by the clergyman and she listened intently to his instructions. Laura waited until she received a nod of

31

agreement and then took off her cloak. Beth picked it up and wrapped it around herself.

"You can take my cloak in exchange," Beth said to Laura. "Yours is better quality than mine, but I'm sure you won't mind the swap."

Laura nodded in agreement. "Thank you for this," she said quietly.

"You're welcome, it is the most excitement I've had for weeks," Beth responded with an impish smile. Her features were sharper than Laura's and although she had a similar hair colour, hers was straight, whereas Laura's held a natural wave. Putting the two women together, a blind man could tell that they were nothing alike, Laura just hoped that the cloak would be enough to convince her pursuer for a little while.

The clergyman interrupted her thoughts. "There is a door here onto the side street. I suggest you take a hackney, but not directly from here. If questions are asked later, you don't want to be easily traced. Good luck and may God be with you," he said, opening the door quietly.

Laura thanked him and left the building as quickly as she could. She had no idea how much of a head start she had, but she had to make every moment count.

The clergyman helped Beth back into the church, pretending that she had become a little faint. "Sit here for a while," he said, more gently than his tone had been previously. "I didn't realise you were in such a poor state."

He had noticed the man had moved forward from the pew he had previously sat on. He entered another pew at the sight of the clergyman and Beth. If there was any action to convince him that Laura was telling the truth, that was it.

The priest sat down near to Beth. He had not intended staying with the young girl, but the movement of the man made him wonder if he would approach her in a church and he did not want to put his staff in danger.

They sat for half an hour before the clergyman roused himself. "Right, Beth, I think you've had enough of a rest for today, don't you? Time to get back to work I think," he said loudly.

Beth stood and took off the cloak, shaking it out and looking all around the church, not focusing on anyone in particular. They both heard a curse and the sound of footsteps, followed by the banging of the church door as the man ran out into the street.

Chapter 4

Laura had run as fast as she was able to in the circumstances. She knew the streets well and took every twist and turn that would take her as far away as possible from the church. Eventually, she paused and caught her breath, before turning into a street, calmly walking up to a hackney and instructing it to take her to the Bow Street Offices.

She alighted from the hackney and paused. She could not walk into the offices, as much as she needed help. The fear of seeing him after all these months, even though he was a decent man, made her falter at the last moment. If he turned her away, she had nowhere left to go. He had every right to cast her off, he owed her nothing. In fact, he had given her money that could help her to get away, but she had been foolish and stayed in familiar surroundings and now she was running for her life.

The day passed with Laura being the person that hid in the shadows, watching the Bow Street Office. She was not sure what would give her the confidence to enter the building, but when she saw Alfred leaving the offices during the early evening, she followed him at a distance.

Alfred seemed relaxed as he walked through the streets towards his home. Laura had no idea where he lived, they had not had such revealing conversation, so she had no clue as to whether the walk would be long or short. She just kept walking, trying to maintain a distance that would keep him in sight, but that would not alert him to the fact that she was there.

He stuck to the main streets, but then Laura lost sight of him. She was no expert in following someone and cursed to herself, obviously the distance she had been keeping from him was too much. As she picked up her pace, an arm from the side of a building grabbed at her. Laura screamed and started to wriggle, panicking that her pursuer had caught up with her after all.

At the sound of her scream, she heard a familiar voice. "What the? Laura?" Alfred asked, letting her go.

"Oh thank God," Laura breathed heavily, leaning against the wall for support. The thought that her escape had been in vain had made her feel weak.

"What on earth do you think you are doing trying to follow me? I could have hurt you," Alfred snapped. He was having trouble gathering himself at the surprise at meeting Laura again in such a way, but he had also felt something else, it had been like a kick to his ribs. When he had dragged her to him, he had felt the swell of her middle.

"I need your help," Laura said weakly.

"Yet you didn't think to come into the offices?" Alfred said sharply.

"I couldn't pluck up the courage," Laura said. Alfred's tone and the cold expression in his eyes did not bode well for him being willing to offer support. "Alfred, I'm sorry….." Laura started, but then slid down the wall. The shock at being grabbed, in addition to not eating all day and the realisation that her potential saviour may not be willing to help her after all, was too much. She suddenly felt very faint and her legs no longer supported her.

"Damn it," Alfred cursed as he hooked his hands under Laura's arms and dragged her to her feet. "Laura, come on, stay awake, I need to get you home."

Laura was half supported, half dragged, down two further streets, before Alfred stopped in front of a lodging house. He sighed as he entered the building, if he was seen by his landlady, he would be homeless by the morning. She took pride in running an honourable house that attracted the right kind of gentleman.

Laura made no sound as they walked up the stairs to the second floor. Alfred had wanted security where he lived, so a visible landlady and a set of rooms at the top of the building had seemed perfect. As he helped Laura, who was leaning heavily on him, he now questioned his sanity with choosing to live at the top of so many stairs.

He opened the door and breathed heavily when he had placed Laura on a wooden chair in the hallway. He closed the door and leaned on the back of it. He had no idea what had happened in the months since he had seen Laura last, but he had an idea that he was not going to like it.

When the colour had returned to Laura's cheeks, he helped her into a small drawing room and placed her on a more comfortable sofa. "Wait here," he instructed and moved to a side room. He had a small area for storing food that did not need keeping in a kitchen. The rooms did not have their own kitchen. His landlady provided the warm meals that he needed.

He brought out some bread and cheese. His unsociable working hours meant that he always had a ready supply of food. In his job, there were very often long periods of time without the opportunity of sourcing food and he would not dare to knock on his landlady's door at two or three of the clock in the night and demand to be fed.

"Eat these," he instructed Laura. "It will make you feel better. I am guessing you haven't eaten for a while."

"Not since last night," Laura admitted, falling onto the food as if she had been starved for a week.

"That isn't good for a woman in your condition," Alfred said, not able to prevent the tone of disapproval in his voice.

Laura paused from eating and met Alfred's gaze. "You must think I am the lowest of the low," she said quietly, losing her appetite at the tone of Alfred's voice.

"I'm in no position to judge you," Alfred replied. It was true, he normally would not judge Laura. She was a lady of the night, most who chose that occupation had no other option, except to starve. He could not condemn someone for trying to survive, even if the consequence were unwanted pregnancies. The reason that it had affected him so much was because she was the only woman who he had ever considered....., ever wished that their lives could have been different. Only their lives were what they were, and although he had a lump of lead in his stomach that felt that it was the size of a large boulder, he would have to accept that Laura had been with other men, many other men.

"I want this baby," Laura responded defensively.

Alfred gritted his teeth. "Is that why you want my help?"

"No!" Laura said. "You gave me enough money for me to support myself and the baby, but there is something else."

"Go on," Alfred said.

He sat down as Laura told him everything that had happened since they had last met. Of the chaos when the property that Baron Kersal had lived in was raided by his colleagues, and how they had all scattered into London. Each had been thankful for the escape, but worried about the future. Even being in a trade such as hers, it had provided security, three meals a day and a roof over her head. For many of the girls, it was better than they had known before.

Laura explained that she had hesitated when thinking about leaving London, it was her home and all she had known. She went on to tell him of the place she had settled in with Clara and the efforts they were making in trying to make a respectable living.

"You had given me money, but I wanted to make sure it lasted and provided for the baby as well," Laura explained, not quite meeting Alfred's eyes.

"What about the father?" Alfred asked, unable to stop himself.

"Would you be happy if a woman of ill-repute came knocking on your door, saying that you were the father of her child?" Laura asked defiantly, but watching closely at the response to her words.

"I probably wouldn't believe her," Alfred replied coldly. He was not normally so emotional, but Laura's condition had caused his insides to twist and turn as thoughts raced through his head. He was being harsh with her, the last person in the world he would normally hurt, but at the moment he could not stop himself.

Laura felt a part of her die at his words, but carried on with her story. She explained how the news that the Baron had walked away a free man had not really affected them, since they had not expected their lives to ever cross again. Then she told him about Sarah and Veronica disappearing.

"Could they not just have left the area?" Alfred asked.

"No," Laura said firmly. "They had nowhere else to go. Veronica certainly did not have any family to go too. I didn't truly believe that they were dead until I saw what happened to Clara though."

She explained what had happened by the side of the Thames. "Was it the first time you had seen the man?" Alfred asked.

"Yes, I think so," Laura said, trying to remember. "The problem is that in the area that we live in, you don't tend to make eye contact with most of the men in the area, as it could cause problems. If he was only following Clara, I wouldn't have noticed him, we weren't together all the time."

"He probably wasn't following her for long anyway," Alfred admitted, more to himself than Laura. "You weren't exactly hiding, so he would have found it easy to track you down."

Laura shuddered at the thought of someone watching them without their knowledge. "If Clara hadn't wanted to wait another day," she said quietly.

"I don't think it would have saved her," Alfred said honestly. "If he was waiting to act, any sign from either of you that you were on the move, would just have made him act sooner. You were lucky that you had the presence of mind to get away."

"Yes and the help of a decent clergyman who believed what I said. He could have easily cast me out," Laura said.

"What now?" Alfred asked. "There is no hope of linking this back to Baron Kersal, if that was what you were hoping."

"Oh no!" Laura said quickly. "I never want to see that man again. I was being selfish. You are the only person in London who knows my background and who I trust. I was hoping you could help me to get away, hire a carriage and put as much distance between me and London as possible. I should have done it as soon as the Runners raided us."

"Yes, you should," Alfred said roughly. He was not being cruel, just practical. "Where are you going to go? Have you any family?"

"No," Laura replied. "It's the reason I know for certain that Veronica did not have any family, we talked a lot about our pasts, they were so similar. I just thought I would use the money you gave me to put as much distance between me and here as I can. I hadn't thought about much beyond that if I'm honest."

"You need to go somewhere where you are sure you will receive support, or you will just swap one set of problems for another," Alfred said. He sat and thought for a while before speaking again. He had thought of most options, some of which he knew were selfish and immediately had to be dismissed. He finally decided that in reality there was only one option that Laura had.

"We shall have to write to Lord Halkyn and ask for his assistance," Alfred said, sure that the peer would give it.

"I know I helped to give information about Baron Kersal, but why would he help now?" Laura asked.

"He will always feel obliged to you because of his wife," Alfred responded, smiling at the expressions that passed over Laura's face as she realised the implications of Alfred's words.

"You mean he........she's gone and.........well I never!" she finally said, half laughing, half shocked.

Alfred smiled, "It seems she was a good match for him. There was no doubt that he was smitten with her from the first time that I met him," Alfred said, remembering the Lord who was determined to seek revenge for the girl who Baron Kersal had tried to wrong. It had only been through Laura's guidance and Lord Halkyn's help that Charlotte Webster had been able to escape.

The result had been that Lord Halkyn, a confirmed bachelor had then fallen in love with the girl. It had not been an easy journey for them, but Alfred had not been surprised when he had received notification of their recent marriage.

"Well I didn't expect that to happen," Laura said. "Who'd have thought that little innocent Charlotte could capture the cold hearted lord?"

"He wasn't very cold and aloof when it was anything to do with Lady Halkyn," Alfred said, remembering the times he had been with Lord Halkyn. The emotions had ranged from raging lord, determined to seek revenge, to drunken wastrel, wallowing in self-pity, when the romance was not going as he hoped.

"Lady Halkyn, how lovely that sounds," Laura said. There was no bitterness in her words, people like Charlotte seemed to deserve happy endings more than her own kind did. "Do you think they would help?"

"There's no reason why they wouldn't. But for you, they would never have met," Alfred responded. "You are only asking for a place to shelter, which, if they knew what has happened, I'm sure they would offer without hesitation."

Laura felt the wave of relief wash over her at the possibility of a solution. "How will I contact them?" she asked.

"I will send a letter, I think it would be better if it came from me," ever the practical Alfred offered. "I will send it to Lord Halkyn's London house, even though I know he is not there. They will know where he is."

"Can you suggest somewhere safe I can stay until we get a reply?" Laura asked.

Alfred paused. He was being foolish he decided, as he uttered the next words. "You are in the safest place. You got here unobserved, and to leave would put you at risk, so you can stay here."

"How can I?" Laura asked, but the jolt of pleasure that had shot through her at Alfred's words was the nicest feeling she had felt in a long time.

"It is going to be difficult," Alfred admitted. "I am going to have to feign illness, otherwise we are going to have Mrs Edwards, my landlady, coming in to clean."

Between them they concocted a plan that although far-fetched, because of Alfred's previous impeccable behaviour, was more likely to be believed.

Chapter 5

Alfred sent off a letter straight away. He was not about to let Laura put herself at risk, but he did realise that the next few days would feel like an eternity. It had been hard enough to keep away from her when he had been working undercover in the Baron's household, but in his own rooms, it would be harder still. He would have to keep reminding himself that she was heavy with another man's child.

He managed to convince his landlady that he was ill and sent round a note to his workplace, to say that he was not well enough to be at work. Once everything was in place all they could do was wait.

Food was still provided for by Mrs Edwards, although it had to be split between two. Alfred tried not to dwell on what she thought when he returned every plate empty, while at the same time complaining that he could barely move due to illness.

Laura busied herself as best she could, but there were few books and even fewer that would interest her. Alfred unsurprisingly did not collect novels. She tried to move around as much as she could, but although the rooms were spacious for a man of Alfred's means, in reality the space was limited. The first day seemed to last an age.

As the evening closed in, Laura sighed, flopping herself on the sofa. "How long do you think it will take to receive a reply?"

Alfred smiled, it was the fourth time she had asked in the last hour. "It depends where they are. It could be days."

"I will be in Bedlam before then!" Laura said dramatically.

"I will go out tonight and see if I can gather anything that will distract us," Alfred said.

"Can I come?" Laura asked eagerly.

"Walking the streets of London, at night, when someone is looking to kill you is a wise plan of action, is it?" Alfred asked sarcastically.

"But I'll be with you," Laura responded.

Alfred paused before speaking, her words had flattered him, in that she had so much faith in him. "It is not safe Laura," he said gently. "I will bring what I can."

Alfred left the house when everything had gone quiet. He was used to coming and going without making a sound, so no one in the other rooms was disturbed. He checked the area once he was outside. He was fairly sure that Laura had not been followed, but it was better to be safe than sorry. He only left when he was sure that Laura would be secure.

He wandered the streets, enjoying the fact of being outside, even if the air was humid. He was not used to being inside so much, so he picked up his pace and burned off some energy before becoming focussed on his tasks.

He visited numerous establishments. Some parts of London never closed, if you knew where to go. He obtained everything he needed and returned to his rooms, being careful to double back and make sure he was not being followed.

He crept in the room and immediately knew that Laura was asleep. There was a stillness to the air that only occurred when everyone in a place was at rest. He had learned to recognise the different atmospheres in a building as part of his training for his job. He placed all his packages in the side room and settled on the sofa. It was going to be an uncomfortable night.

Laura woke as first light entered the room. She had not closed the curtains, for fear of being seen near the window. She lay in the sunlight, slowly going through the previous day's events. She stretched and climbed out of bed. She had hung her dress as best she could, to try and get the creases to drop out, but it would not be many days before she looked like a waif off the streets.

She entered the drawing room and stopped at the sight of Alfred lying on the sofa. He looked uncomfortable and she felt guilty at preventing him from having his own bed. She moved slowly across the room, but even though she had been careful, Alfred awoke at her movements.

"Good morning," he said groggily, sitting up and rubbing his hands over his face.

"You look awful," Laura said with sympathy.

"It will help me to be more believable then," Alfred croaked. "There are books on the table that you may be interested in."

Laura picked up the books in wonder. Novels! He had chosen well, Fanny Burney, Maria Edgeworth, in addition to some by unnamed authors, plus books of poetry, Byron, Wordsworth and Shelley. He had also managed to obtain some periodicals. At least the second day would not seem as long as the first one had.

"I've also got more food and drink. It isn't hot, but I think it would be more convincing if I sent some of my dishes back with some food remaining on them to Mrs Edwards. She is more likely to believe that I am ill, that way," Alfred said.

"Yes, but her cooking is so good," Laura said longingly.

Alfred smiled, "Control yourself, woman!"

Laura tutted at his cheek and walked into the side room. The worktop was covered in bread, cheeses, hams and cold pie. There were also flagons of small beer. "You have been busy, I'm surprised you managed to carry all this home," she said with approval. "Are you preparing for a siege?"

"We don't know how long we will need to remain here, so thought it was best to keep the need to leave my rooms at a minimum," Alfred said, entering the room and tearing off a piece of bread.

"I was hoping that you would receive a reply today," Laura said, her buoyant mood fading a little.

Alfred smiled, "Lord and Lady Halkyn are possibly still away after their wedding, it could be a few days."

Laura settled herself down and read for the morning. She hid in the side room whenever Mrs Edwards knocked on the door to deliver food. Alfred always asked her to leave it outside the room, his excuse being that he did not wish his landlady to catch whatever malady he had.

In the afternoon, she became unsettled again. She was not used to being so confined. Even at Baron Kersal's she had the days to herself, as gentlemen usually spent the days with their families. They only visited during the evenings when they wanted to explore the seedier side of life with the women of the night.

Laura started to pace around the room. Alfred watched her for a while without speaking. She had left her hair down and she looked every bit the trapped tigress as she prowled around his drawing room.

"Would you like a game of cards?" Alfred asked, trying to divert them both. He did not like the way his body still reacted to Laura, even though she was with child.

"I suppose so," Laura said, sitting opposite him.

"Your enthusiasm is heart-warming," Alfred said drily.

"I'm not very good company, am I?" Laura asked with a smile. "I am grateful for what you are doing you know, even though I may not sound like I am."

"Anyone would have helped you," Alfred said, brushing off the compliment.

"No, I know a lot of people, although few of them well," Laura said, picking up the cards that Alfred had dealt. "But there was only you that I knew I could trust."

"Dependable Alfred eh? Doesn't sound like much of a recommendation," Alfred said with a grimace.

"Believe me, it is the highest recommendation I could ever give someone," Laura said with feeling. "Anyway, you get your excitement from your job, I would have thought that you would want a quiet life when you return home."

"I do," Alfred responded truthfully.

Laura looked at her protector. "You are a man of many faces aren't you?"

"What do you mean?" Alfred asked. He did not particularly like the focus of attention being on himself, but he did wish to know what Laura thought of him.

"You obviously are very good at your job and enjoy the dangerous aspect of it," Laura responded, seeming to study Alfred as she spoke. "But you are also very considerate. You're helping me when you could have sent me on my way, even though it is inconveniencing you and maybe even putting you in danger. You are also very gentle."

"Gentle?" Alfred spluttered. "I've never been called that before."

"You were gentle with me in Baron Kersal's house," Laura said, pleased that she had made the controlled Alfred look uncomfortable.

"That was in the past," Alfred said, not wishing to be reminded of one of the best nights of his life, even if it had been spent in the arms of a woman he had paid for. "Your turn," he said, trying to draw Laura back to the game of cards.

They played game after game until the evening drew in and they needed to light candles. Laura set out some food and they sat comfortably on the sofa next to each other. They munched quietly for a while, before Laura placed down her plate, content for a while.

"So what do your family think of your job?" She asked.

"They don't know," Alfred said with a shrug.

"What?" Laura responded in surprise. "How would they feel if something happened to you and they hadn't even known that you worked for Bow Street?" She knew how she would feel if anything had happened to him, and she knew what his job was.

"They would probably think that I had got the end that I deserved," Alfred said, his brow furrowing.

"No!" Laura exclaimed in surprise. "How could someone think that of you? You are the most decent person I have ever known," she said forcefully.

"Well I pity you," Alfred said with genuine feeling. "You have seen me three times Laura, you know nothing about me, don't fool yourself into thinking that you do."

Laura reached over and cupped his cheek with her hand. She could feel the stubble that was developing as the day reached its close. "I've had to have the ability to read people quickly and although I admit that I have only been in your company a few times, I know this for a certainty Alfred, you are a decent man, so you can stop trying to convince me otherwise."

Alfred closed his eyes for a second, enjoying her touch, before collecting himself and moving away from her hand. "You know nothing, Laura," he said quietly and moved away from her.

Laura remained seated and watched as Alfred kicked at the cinders in the hearth. She wondered about the man standing before her, admitting that it was true that she knew very little about him. She was sure that her conviction was right though, he was a good man. Whatever secrets he hid, they had not corrupted him as they could have done, and he was risking his life every day to keep others safe.

Alfred cursed to himself as he stood, glaring down at the fire. He should never have let her into his rooms. She was a danger to him, because despite everything, he wanted her. Since meeting Laura, he had dreamed of a life that was beyond his reach, one in which he was a husband, had a wife with fiery red hair and they lived a decent life. Not one that virtually guaranteed that neither would reach old age, accepting that both had done things in the past that would make decent people shudder. She made him want what he could never have, and he cursed her for it.

Chapter 6

Neither Alfred nor Laura spoke until it was time to retire to bed. Both had been engrossed in their own private thoughts. Laura was the first to break the silence. "I didn't know that doing nothing all day could be so exhausting," she said with a yawn and a stretch.

Alfred smiled slightly, "Yes, the jobs where I am observing, leave me shattered at the end of my duty and very often I haven't moved. Take the bed and I will see you in the morning."

"You can't sleep on this sofa again," Laura said, standing up. "It's barely comfortable to sit on all day, it must be a nightmare to sleep on it."

Alfred did not know whether to laugh or to be annoyed. "It's not very polite to criticise the standard of your sanctuary."

Laura grinned, "Is it a criticism, or is it that I'm speaking the truth?"

Alfred smirked, "Well whatever it is, the sofa is going to be my bed."

"Why are you being so prudish?" Laura asked, "You weren't the last time we met."

Alfred scowled at the woman stood before him. Damn her for constantly reminding him of that last time. "Yes, but things have changed slightly since then, haven't they?" he responded, making the glance at her swollen stomach, a pointed look.

Laura flushed, "I wasn't offering you anything more than a comfortable bed!" she snapped, embarrassed and hurt at Alfred's harshness. "We have shared a bed before, why not have a comfortable night's sleep? Neither of us is an innocent."

He had hurt her and he was sorry the way he made snide comments to her about her condition. He was not being fair, he knew that. The problem was though, that it was a constant reminder to him that she had been with other men. He knew that it was unreasonable for him to react to her in such a way, it was a consequence of her job, but he could not stop himself. He had not been with another woman since he had first met her, no one had drawn him like she had.

Her words were sensible though. They need not be impractical, and there was not any reason why they should not share a bed. "Fine, as long as you truly don't mind and promise not to take up the whole of the bed," he muttered trying to lighten the mood.

Laura recovered quickly from her mortification and responded to Alfred in kind. "You are a sliver of a man, you shouldn't need more than a corner anyway. There isn't an ounce of meat on you."

"There won't be, what with needing to starve myself while pretending that I'm ill," Alfred said, smacking her on the backside as she walked into the bedchamber. "Take up too much room and I'll push you onto the floor."

"Don't ever go undercover as a gentleman, you would be useless at it," Laura responded, looking over her shoulder.

They continued to banter until they were under the covers. Both had kept some clothing on, Laura, her chemise and Alfred had his breeches. Although it was the right decision to share the bed, there was obviously no use in putting too much temptation in each other's way.

Alfred was disturbed from a dreamless sleep by small moans coming from Laura. At first he had thought that there must be something wrong with the baby, but it soon became apparent that she was having a bad dream. It was no surprise really, Alfred thought to himself. If he knew that someone was determined to kill him, he was not sure that he would rest easy.

He tried to shake Laura gently, but it only succeeded in making her more disturbed. Alfred groaned to himself, he could not leave her upset, so he started to stroke her face gently, whispering her name. It was a few moments before she slowly opened her eyes, almost as if she was frightened to do so.

"Alfred?" she asked, seeing his face close to hers. "What's wrong?"

"Shh," came the soothing voice. "You were having a nightmare."

"I couldn't reach you in time," Laura said quietly, she looked afraid and vulnerable.

"I'm here, nothing is going to happen," Alfred said, taking Laura into his arms and holding her close. "Go back to sleep, all is well."

*

Laura awoke to the sensation of feeling wrapped up and secure. Alfred's arms were holding her tightly as he slept, his body folded around hers from behind. She remembered being woken up during her nightmare and smiled to herself. He could say what he wished, but his actions proved even further that he was a decent man.

She lay perfectly still, this was the place where she wanted to be. If only it could last, if only it was happening for a different reason.

Alfred moaned in his sleep and moved his hand, it brushed her breast and he squeezed it, half asleep. Laura remained still, his touch made her insides stir, but she dared not move in case she woke Alfred. Laura knew the second he reached consciousness, because his hand stilled before moving carefully away from her. He withdrew and sat up on the edge of the bed, rubbing his hands through his hair and over his face.

"Morning," Laura said, turning over to face his back and stretching.

"Laura...," Alfred started.

"Don't say anything, it was a nice way to wake up," she said rubbing her hand gently across his back. Alfred turned slightly and looked at her. Laura smiled at him in reassurance. "Well I thought it was, anyway," she said with a wink.

Alfred stood and laughed at her, the seriousness of his mood gone. "You will be the death of me woman, I hope Lord Halkyn replies soon."

Laura remained on the bed until Alfred had washed and dressed. She had mixed feelings, she knew that they could not remain as they were indefinitely, but she could not deny that being so close with Alfred was the best thing that had ever happened to her.

During the day, Laura kept up the banter. She had decided that Alfred was far too serious for his own good and although she was in a precarious situation, humour had always got her through such situations before. So she teased and tormented him at every opportunity. She also touched him whenever she could. Each time it could be excused as accidental, but she used every opportunity to her advantage. The truth was that since she had woken up in his arms, she had wanted him.

Alfred was being driven to distraction, although he felt a little like a moth drawn to a flame. She was being funny, teasing, annoying, and oh so tempting. He could almost scream with frustration as she brushed against him again and again. The problem was, it was all done with so much humour and fun that he could not chastise her. He had never smiled as much in his life as he did that day, and his cheeks ached because of it. He was usually so serious and steady, able to keep his emotions in check, except when he was around Laura.

Late on in the afternoon she punched him as a response to something he had said and he grabbed her arm. "You aren't being very nice to your rescuer," Alfred responded, holding onto her arm at the wrist.

Laura used the contact to roll herself into his arms. "I can be nice if my rescuer wishes."

Alfred stilled at the movement. He was so tempted, but his conscience would not let him. "Things have changed, Laura," he said quietly.

"I am still me," Laura said, seeing the battle going on within Alfred and reaching up with her free hand to brush back his hair gently. "Why not allow yourself to do what you want, and I know you want to, Alfred."

Alfred closed his eyes, "I can't Laura," he said quietly, but firmly. "You are carrying a child, I can't, no matter how much I may want to."

Laura blinked back tears, "No matter how much I want you to?" she asked.

"I'm sorry Laura. I can't," Alfred responded, moving out of her touch, all the pleasure of the day gone. "I have to ask, would you not receive support from the father if he knew of your predicament? I have presumed not, with you coming to me, but maybe he would offer protection," Alfred needed to get her away from him before he weakened, which wouldn't be very long if the days continued the way they had today.

"If I was honest and told the father about the baby, he would not believe me," Laura said, sitting down and not looking at Alfred.

The pain etched on Laura's face, tore at Alfred's insides. She must have thought highly of the father, he thought. He had the sudden need to get some fresh air. "I am going to visit Lord Halkyn's address and see if there is anything that I can find out," he said, moving to put on his frock coat. "I shall be back as quickly as I can."

Laura was left alone, to come to terms with Alfred's rejection. It was no real surprise that he had turned away from her, a man so steadfast would not want to bed a woman who was heavy with another man's child. She sighed to herself, if only she could be brave enough to say the words, perhaps he would believe her and everything would be well.

She almost laughed at her foolish thoughts. Believe her? He had made it quite clear that he would not believe her if she told him the truth. People like her did not get happy endings, she had known that from a very early age. If she felt any sorrow, she only had herself to blame. She had never expected to be in contact with Alfred again when she had wished for a part of him. God had granted her wish, but it came with a catch; the father of her child was constantly rejecting her, and had told her clearly that he would not believe a woman of the night if she told him she was pregnant with his child.

The irony that Alfred was not only protecting her, but his own child and would never know that it was his, made her cry until the light outside had completely faded.

Chapter 7

Alfred walked to Lord Halkyn's house on Belgrave Square. It was a substantial walk from where he lived, but he needed the exercise to burn off the frustration that spending so much time in Laura's company had caused.

He could have easily bedded her. He wanted to more than anything else, but how could he have faced her or himself afterwards? No, he would help her and then leave her. He just hoped he could contact Lord Halkyn soon.

Alfred arrived at the house and groaned when he saw the knocker was removed. Why could life not be simple sometimes and have the person he needed to speak to in residence? He made his way through the wrought iron fencing that surrounded the basement area and walked down the steps. He knocked on the tradesman's door and waited. Every house left staff to maintain the house whilst its family was away.

The door was opened by a young scullery maid. "Yes Sir?" she asked.

"Is the butler available?" Alfred remembered that Lord Halkyn had used his butler's given name, but it was not appropriate that a visitor to the house took the same liberty.

"Who shall I tell him is calling?"

"Tell him Mr Peters," Alfred said.

He was left to stand in the basement area, until a few moments later the butler opened the door and welcomed him inside.

"Good evening, Mr Peters, this is an unexpected pleasure," Walter said, as cool and calm as always.

"Good evening, I was wondering if I could have a word with you in private?" Alfred asked. He did not want the staff overhearing any part of what he had to say.

"Certainly Sir, if you would follow me," Walter said, leading the way down a stone corridor.

Rooms led off the corridor, all conducive to the smooth running of a large house, Walter continued until he reached the butler's pantry. He led the way inside and closed the door once Alfred had entered. The room had a small fireplace in the corner, which was giving out a welcoming glow. A chair was placed at either side of the fireplace, obviously the location where the butler rested, if ever the opportunity arose. The walls were filled with shelves and cupboards, some of which were locked, probably containing some of the more expensive pieces of the dining silver. In the centre of the room was a large wooden table, showing signs of being well scrubbed over the years. It was a room that felt warm, but was very much a practical space.

Walter indicated that Alfred should take a seat on one of the chairs near the fire. "Would you like a glass of port Mr Peters? One of the advantages to working for Lord Halkyn is that he gives a generous allowance in port and wine for his senior staff."

Alfred smiled slightly, "Yes please. You will have to excuse me, I'm afraid I only know you as Walter and not your family name. Lord Halkyn was always very familiar with you when I was in his company."

Walter smiled, a smile full of affection. "Yes, since I was a young footman, Lord Halkyn has used my given name and so when I was fortunate enough to be promoted to butler, it just seemed odd reverting to a more formal address. Using Walter is fine, sometimes I forget I have another name, except when working with the younger staff of course."

"Of course," Alfred said, accepting the glass of port. He remembered clearly the easy relationship that existed between the butler and the Lord. It was obvious that the butler had helped his employer out of many situations, the way Walter was prone to offer solutions. He was not surprised though, that although seeming to be one of the more relaxed members of his profession, with the other staff, he was still as formal as his peers.

"How may I help you?" Walter asked, after both men had taken a sip of their port and savoured the quality of it.

"I sent a letter a few days ago to Lord Halkyn and although I realise he is away from London, I wondered if you had any idea how quickly I would receive a response?" Alfred explained.

"Ah, there may be an unusual delay with regards to any reply," Walter responded.

Alfred's heart sank, "Why?"

"You are aware of Lord Halkyn's recent marriage?" Walter asked. He continued when Alfred nodded in acknowledgement. "They have taken an extended wedding trip. Apparently Lady Halkyn had travelled so little prior to her marriage, that Lord Halkyn was determined to show her England, Scotland and Wales." The words were said with approval. Walter had been delighted that the quiet Miss Webster he had first met on that strange night not so long ago, had been the one to tame his unruly master. It had been a further confirmation of Lord Halkyn's affection when he had troubled himself to arrange such a long tour for the pleasure of his wife. He had been determined to give her a trip that would delight her.

"I thought they may still be on a tour after their marriage," Alfred said. "I am surprised that it would cause such a delay though, they surely are receiving letters only a few days after they are delivered here?" Alfred knew full well the efficiency of the postal system that seemed to be able to track anyone down, anywhere in the country, almost in a matter of hours.

"Normally, yes," Walter acknowledged, his face showing some amusement. "But Lord Halkyn said that he had wasted far too much time and was going to make every moment count with Lady Halkyn. He said that if anyone dared to contact them, unless there was flood, an invasion of locusts, or famine, they would receive no reference when he dismissed them." The words had been uttered in Lord Halkyn's usual forceful way and although at the time Walter had maintained his composure and assured his Lordship that there would be no disturbances, he had grinned all the way to the kitchen. His master was in love and long may it continue.

"Damn," Alfred said, sinking back into the chair, deflated.

"Is there a problem I can assist with?" Walter asked.

"It's probably better if you don't know the details. Someone is at risk and I was hoping with the work that I had done with Lord Halkyn in the past, that he could offer assistance. It is clear that he can't, not at the moment at least," Alfred said, trying to sound calmer than he felt. He did not have a network of people outside London that he could send Laura to for safety, it was becoming apparent to him that she had picked the wrong man to help her.

"I am sorry, but even if I forwarded your letter on, he probably would just throw it in the nearest fire. He has a history of doing that," Walter said, remembering with a shudder the time when his master had gone into such a decline that he had feared for him.

"I suppose I shall have to wait until they return," Alfred said in resignation. "I just hope they tire of travelling soon." It was a vain hope, but the only thing he had.

Alfred said his goodbyes to the butler and walked up the stairs from the basement as if he had the world's worries on his shoulders. He could not continue the farce about him being ill indefinitely. There would come a point when his landlady would demand access to his room and then they would be discovered. He could not protect Laura in London, he had no idea to what extent the Baron would go to in trying to find her. If he had arranged the killing of three women already, he was obviously a determined man, so while she remained in London, Laura was in danger.

Alfred sighed at the top of the steps. He could not dally, they would have to make alternative plans and quickly. He needed to return to his lodgings. As he walked across the square, leaving Lord Halkyn's house behind him, a carriage swung around and stopped at one of the houses of the opposite side. At first Alfred did not take much notice of the carriage, but then something caught his eye and he picked up his pace.

The carriage was adorned with the Dunham crest and Lord Dunham was alighting from it. Alfred hurried to catch Lord Dunham before he entered his house, since he would probably not be receiving visitors at this hour. So, although it went against every instruction in polite behaviour, Alfred interrupted Lord Dunham and his companion on the steps of the house.

"Lord Dunham!" Alfred said.

Lord Dunham turned, not looking pleased at his conversation being interrupted. He looked closely at the gentleman stood on the pavement, before a look of recognition passed across his face. "Mr Peters?" he asked in surprise.

"Yes my Lord," Alfred said with relief. The first hurdle was overcome, there had been no guarantee that Lord Dunham would remember him. "I am sorry to prey on you at this hour, but would it be possible to have a private word with you?"

"Now?" Lord Dunham asked, not unfriendly, but not overly welcoming either.

"If it wasn't of importance my Lord, I would not be interrupting your evening. I've been trying to contact Lord Halkyn, but without success. It appears he has gone to ground and is not available for communication," Alfred explained.

The message to anyone other than Lord Dunham sounded cryptic at best, but Lord Dunham inclined his head slightly and indicated that Alfred should join him. So, with a sigh of relief from Alfred, the three gentlemen entered the house.

The black and white marble hallway was a far cry from the servant's entrance that Alfred had been led down a few minutes previously. The staircase swept up from the ground floor, leading the way enticingly to the higher rooms. Solid oak doors, stood to attention around the edge of the hallway, to which Lord Dunham led the way to one.

"Dawson, I'll see you in the drawing room, after I've spoken to Mr Peters," Lord Dunham said to his friend.

Alfred was ushered into the study and admired the richness of the wood and amount of books adorning the shelves. The chairs that were in this room, were not the wooden chairs, filled with cushions that had been in the butler's pantry, but the high winged-back, upholstered chairs that promised both comfort and warmth.

Lord Dunham sat at his desk and indicated that Alfred should take the chair opposite him. "I'm presuming this has something to do with Baron Kersal?" He asked, correctly guessing that any contact between the Bow Street Officer and Lord Halkyn would be to do with the case they had worked on together.

"It has, my Lord," Alfred replied. "I am sorry about the intrusion, but seeing your carriage gave a glimmer of hope in an otherwise very dark evening."

Alfred explained about Laura's approach and what his intentions had been. He explained their current predicament and the loss that he was at since he had undertaken his evening enquiries at Lord Halkyn's home.

Lord Dunham sat, thinking for a few moments before responding to the story. "Do you believe everything this Laura tells you?" he asked.

"I do," Alfred said without hesitation. "She is not an hysterical female, or a conniving one, I know her profession may lead people to mistrust what she is saying, but she has never lied to us before. She has asked for nothing, apart from help to reach safety."

"Trust Halkyn to refuse to have any contact with the outside world," Lord Dunham muttered to himself. "Is there no one that she knows outside the city?"

"No, people like her tend to have quite a narrow acquaintance, none of who would be willing to acknowledge her during daylight hours," Alfred said, his face betraying nothing.

Lord Dunham looked amused at the officer's words. "Quite so, well it looks like we need to get her away and sooner rather than later," he responded decisively.

Alfred smiled, a rare and genuine smile. "Thank you my Lord."

"There's no need to thank me, she risked herself when she helped Miss Webster, uh, Lady Halkyn, and her evidence brought a stop to the practice, even though Kersal managed to escape the noose. It is only right she is helped in return now, as it would be unfair to leave her to her own fate."

"She is quite independent and once away I am sure will require no further assistance," Alfred assured Lord Dunham, recalling Laura telling him that she still had most of the money that he had given her, as well as her own savings. "There is another problem though, she is heavy with child and there is no sign of the father."

Lord Dunham frowned slightly. "Well that comes as no real surprise, although it does complicate matters further, she needs to be somewhere that she can have the child in safety, before setting up a home. I'm presuming the poor child will be some aristocracy by-blow," Lord Dunham said with sadness and a touch of anger. He had been no angel when enjoying his single days, but he had always taken care to ensure there was no consequences from his liaisons. The fact that he had been motivated by personal reasons made no difference, children could be prevented.

"I have not asked and she has not offered any information," Alfred said stiffly.

Lord Dunham sighed, "Let us be honest, she may not even know who the father is, if she was a popular girl."

Alfred was unable to reply, as he was gritting his teeth so hard. That was an image he was fighting almost every moment of every day and he did not appreciate such an open reminder of it, even though it was not an unreasonable assumption.

Lord Dunham did not seem to notice the lull and carried on, "I am returning to Somerset tomorrow, I shall send a letter after I have spoken to my wife and man of business. I have an idea, but need to think it through before committing to it."

"Thank you my Lord, your help is appreciated," Alfred said, rising to his feet. "I shall leave my card with my address on and await your letter."

"Don't worry Peters, it won't be long," Lord Dunham assured him.

Chapter 8

Somerset 1816

Lord Dunham had sent letters ahead of his return home. He realised that time was of the utmost importance and although he would have preferred to have spoken face to face to those involved, he needed to move things along. Once the letters arrived, it would start the conversations that needed to be held and hopefully he could finalise everything on the first night that he arrived back.

He travelled as fast as he could to reach Dunham House, not because of wishing to help Laura, but because every moment spent away from his darling Elizabeth and baby girl, was a moment too many. The horses were changed as quickly as possible and the stopovers were taken, but the carriage was on the road again before many of the inhabitants in each inn they stopped at, had even realised that morning had arrived.

The carriage reached the open doorway of Dunham House and Phelps was there to greet him, as always. The footman let down the steps in the carriage and the butler took Lord Dunham's hat, cane and gloves.

"Good afternoon my Lord," the butler greeted him.

"Good afternoon Phelps, her Ladyship?" Lord Dunham asked. It was the only question he needed answering, where his wife was.

"In your study my Lord." The staff knew not to disturb Lord and Lady Dunham after a separation had occurred, it was an unwritten rule that the couple could share a greeting without interruptions, before business once more took priority. They were out of the ordinary in aristocratic circles in that they loved one another and were far better together than apart.

Over the evening meal, Lord Dunham talked over the issue with Lady Dunham, Mr Anderton, and Miss Fairfield. "Laura needs to leave London as soon as possible, what do you think of my idea?" Lord Dunham asked the people surrounding him.

"She needs to be safe, it's a good plan and it means that she can remain in Yorkshire on the estate, until after the baby is born," Elizabeth, Lady Dunham said. She was a woman who was always practical, and particularly wanting to help the woman she had never met, because of Laura's previous support of her friend Charlotte. "There is only one flaw in your plan."

"Only one?" Lord Dunham asked with a twinkle in his eye. Since the moment he had met his wife she had challenged him in every way and he loved her because of it. Although sometimes she was not as infallible as she thought, nearly losing Lord and Lady Halkyn as friends when she had interfered with their developing romance.

Elizabeth smiled at her husband. "Yes, only one, although it is a large flaw," she said, looking smug.

Lord Dunham groaned, "Go on, tell me the error of my ways."

"She can't travel with Charles, it wouldn't be fair to her in her condition," Elizabeth said, sympathetic to anyone increasing since she still had very recent memories of it herself.

"I'd presumed Mr Peters would accompany her, he seems very steady and they are obviously friends of sorts now. It never crossed my mind that he would just hand her over to us, I had not discussed it with him, but had supposed that he would want to see her settled," Lord Dunham countered.

"She will need female support, neither Charles nor Mr Peters can be there when the baby arrives," Elizabeth said, knowledgably. "Martha, I know this is out of the ordinary to ask this of you, but would you consider accompanying Charles and settling Laura in? I think she would feel better for it, she must be terrified."

"Me?" Martha spluttered. She blushed as she realised that because the request had been so unexpected, her response had squeaked out. She was not a woman that squeaked. She tried to calm herself down by taking a drink, but she looked mortified.

Elizabeth laughed at the expression on her companion's face. "You have been like a mother to me over the years and I can think of no one better to offer someone support, when it is really needed," she said honestly.

Martha blushed at the compliment. "Thank you, but what about the running of the house?" she asked. She took her job very seriously, it had been a lot to learn when she had started, only having helped to manage a smaller house previously, but through hard work, she had gained the respect of the staff and ran an efficient household.

"It's a perfect opportunity to give one of the under-maids the chance to help to run a large house. We were planning a visit to Violet and Edward in London, sometime soon. We could bring that visit forward, so there would be little work to be done while we are gone," Elizabeth explained. She may not enjoy visiting the capital, but sometimes it would be necessary and Lord Dunham's sister and brother-in-law were very dear to her.

"Oh, I see," Martha responded, not liking what she was hearing.

Elizabeth quickly reached over and squeezed the hand of her long-time companion. "Martha, don't think for one moment that this is anything but the highest compliment to you, there is no other woman I would want by my side when I was in trouble, or needed support. She needs you," she said, genuinely sorry that her companion should feel the request was anything other than the highest praise.

"I don't mean to make a fuss," Martha said quickly, her cheeks burning at such focus of attention on herself. "Of course I will do as you wish."

"Good. Excellent," Lord Dunham responded. "I will send off a letter this evening and if you both could be ready by tomorrow afternoon, it would be best to leave then. You have a long journey before you, with the need to go to London first."

Charles and Martha both nodded their agreement. The small group broke up soon after, Lord Dunham to write his letter to Alfred, while Charles and Martha needed to give instructions to other staff members who would be responsible for tasks in their absence, and they also needed to pack. There was no indication at the moment when they would be returning.

Charles had watched the interchange between Martha and Lady Dunham with a mixture of feelings. He had initially been amused at Martha's reaction, anything that ruffled her made him smile. After that first moment though, the reality of the situation sank in, he would not have his escape from Martha Fairfield after all. That was really a mixed blessing. He liked her a lot, but the way he had been managing to anger her recently did not bode well for a long journey, or a lengthy stay when there would not be the same level of work involved as there was at Dunham House. Suddenly, the next few weeks seemed a little daunting. He was no coward, but he did not want to antagonise the woman further than he had done already.

Martha met Charles coming out of the kitchen. She had spent the last hour with Cook, passing over some of her duties. It was fortunate that Lady Dunham had suggested that the family would be travelling to London, as it reduced the level of work required from the staff.

Charles was approaching the kitchen, when Martha emerged from behind the green baize door. He bowed slightly and stepped to the side to let her pass.

Martha looked at the man before her. He looked confident and perfectly at ease with the situation, while she, although believing the words that Elizabeth had said, (her mistress was no liar), but she still stung from the thought of being sent away from her rightful place. This was an uncharacteristically poor thought from Martha, which was added to by her blaming Charles for the situation.

"I won't forget this in a hurry, Mr Anderton," Martha whispered as she passed Charles. She may be angry with him, but it would not be wise to let the other staff know. Gossip between the staff about other members of staff was avoided if at all possible, especially the senior staff. It only made their positions more difficult.

"What do you mean?" Charles replied in genuine puzzlement and surprise. He had not expected to be exchanging pleasantries, but he had not expect to be spoken to with such venom.

"If you didn't keep undermining me at every opportunity, I would not be being sent away now!" she whispered angrily.

"What? I had nothing to do with it!" Charles exclaimed, astounded that he was being accused of such a crime.

"You have been quick to point out my shortcomings at every possible opportunity, the result being that they no longer have faith in me," Martha continued. "If you hadn't criticised me in the most public of ways, I'm sure her Ladyship would never have suggested such a scheme."

"Lady Dunham said that you were the best person for the job," Charles tried to defend himself. "Her reasons were sensible, I saw no great scheme to undermine you, tonight or any other night. It is all in your imagination."

"I wouldn't expect you to think anything else, other than it was my imagination, or twisted viewpoint. I know your low opinion of me, but you are wrong! I won't now be employing the nanny will I?" Martha snapped. "So, I'm obviously good enough for before the baby is born, but not once it arrives!" She walked away with a stiff back and her head held high, while Charles was left standing open mouthed at her retreating figure.

He had never thought for one moment that she had taken such a dislike to him, but after that outburst, she appeared to detest him. All his previous thoughts about Martha having some feeling for him had disappeared during her tirade, and he was left with the remorse of realising the consequence of his foolish actions. The one woman who he thought about for much of the day, disliked him with all of her being. It was going to be a long trip. A very long trip indeed.

Chapter 9

London

Alfred and Laura had not fallen back into their easy companionship after Laura had tried to persuade Alfred to give in to his feelings. Laura had been hurt by the rejection and Alfred refused to let himself to get into such a position where his weakness would show again. He did not blame Laura, they both had feelings for each other, which had been obvious almost from the moment they had met, but as he had told her, things had changed.

So, an uneasy pact had developed in which they avoided each other as much as possible in the small space of Alfred's lodgings. It helped that Alfred tried to stay out of his rooms as much as possible. On one of his excursions out he decided that he needed to speak to his senior officer and explain what was happening. It was a difficult interview, as he had been absent from his position, without a just cause.

"I could dismiss you," Mr Frost said quietly, after listening to Alfred's explanation.

"I understand if you choose to, sir," Alfred responded, sitting squarely in his seat. He was trying not to let show just what it would mean if he lost his position.

"I took a leap of faith when I appointed you, Peters," Mr Frost said, his voice not betraying whether he was disappointed or angry.

"I know sir, and I appreciate what you did for me before I started my employment," Alfred responded, acknowledging something from his past that he would rather forget.

"I suppose it shows that my faith in you was justified since you have not turned the woman away, and protected her, in a fashion," the calm voice said. "But you will only be a true officer when you learn to rely on your fellow colleagues. By working together we can help each other, if you had the support of the rest of the team, you would not have had to spend so much time locked away."

Alfred smiled a slight smile. "That would have been a help certainly. I suppose I just reacted to the situation when she followed me. My first aim was to get her to safety," he explained.

"Your actions probably saved her life," Mr Frost said. "The team working will come with time. I sometimes forget how short a time you have been with us, because you are so efficient."

"Thank you sir," Alfred said, flushing at the praise.

"So, I suppose while you are so far involved, it just is down to me to give you permission to accompany this young woman to Yorkshire and make sure she is safe," Mr Frost said.

"I don't know how long I will be, I understand if you want to replace me sir," Alfred offered, holding himself stiff in an effort to absorb the blow if it came.

"Take as much time as you need, and we will welcome you when you return," Mr Frost said, reassuringly.

"Thank you Sir, I really appreciate it," Alfred said with one of his rare smiles.

"You're welcome, now get out of my office and sort yourself out. I will tell everyone that you have a sick relative in the North and won't be back for some time," Mr Frost said, and watched as his officer left his office. He wondered if he would see the young man again, although he hoped not to.

Although Alfred did not realise it, the chance to get out of London, was an opportunity to once and for all leave his old life behind. Mr Frost hoped sincerely that Alfred would find a life outside of the city and become the man that he had seen glimpses of during his acquaintance. For Alfred's sake he hoped so, although he would miss the serious young man.

The evening arrived that Alfred and Laura were to be collected. Both waited nervously in the lodgings, until Mr Anderton knocked on the door. Alfred opened the door and let the gentleman in. He remembered Mr Anderton from the time when he had been asked to help Lord Dunham by Lord Halkyn in protecting Lady Dunham. When he had arrived at Dunham House, Lady Dunham was safe, but there was chaos because Miss Webster had been missing. Alfred had taken control and set out to search for her and he had been successful, although she had been injured.

"Good evening Mr Peters," Mr Anderton said. "We have the carriage waiting outside. This is Miss Fairfield, who I'm sure you remember from your visit to Dunham House."

Miss Fairfield followed Mr Anderton into the room and dropped a curtsey. "Mr Peters, it is good to see you again, but I just wish it was under better circumstances."

Alfred, bowed to the two visitors and then turned to Laura, "This is Miss Atkinson. Miss Atkinson, please allow me to introduce, Mr Anderton and Miss Fairfield."

Laura blushed, being introduced as a Miss when obviously expecting a child. It was a slur on the character of a woman to be in such a position and she felt mortified in front of two people who although also employees, were definitely of a higher class than herself. "Good evening, please call me Laura," she said. She had never been known as Miss Atkinson, it hinted at a life she could only dream of.

"In that case, I'm Martha and this is Charles," Martha said, much to the surprise of Mr Anderton. Martha caught his surprised glance. "We've already been travelling for days and are going to be travelling for many more, so there is little point in keeping up the formalities," she responded defensively.

"I'm happy with you using Charles whenever you wish," Charles said with a smile, but the glower he received in return prevented him from getting carried away with thinking that he was gaining any ground with Martha.

Their journey had been a tense few days, Martha only spoke when she was spoken to, and encouraged no further interactions. At the inns where they stayed, she ate with Charles and then immediately retired to her bed. Never had Charles been so glad to see the outskirts of London in his life. He had felt as if the journey had taken weeks, instead of days.

"In that case, please use my given name, Alfred," Alfred offered, feeling a little strange at such familiarity on so short an acquaintance.

"Shall we make our way?" Charles enquired.

"If I could just have a word with you outside first?" Alfred asked. Charles nodded and Alfred led the way downstairs and left the building, needing to speak to the man of business without being overheard.

When the gentlemen had left, Martha turned to her new acquaintance. "Are you well my dear? It must have been difficult remaining indoors for so many days," she said, returning to the kind person that she was, once her nemesis was absent.

"When we arrive in Yorkshire, I don't think I will step inside for a sen'night," Laura said with feeling. "I imagine Alfred is just making sure there is no one loitering outside. I'm sure there isn't. He has been so thorough in protecting me that I have never felt so safe."

"That is good, he seemed like a capable man the last time I met him," Martha said. "Soon we will be on our way and then you can really relax. The estate is lovely and a little out of the way, so people passing through the area don't seem to find it. That's one of the reasons Lady Dunham was attracted to it in the first instance," Martha chatted.

"Everyone has been so very kind," Laura said, a little overwhelmed. "I can never repay what is being done for me."

"You paid in advance when you helped Lady Halkyn," Martha reassured her. "Her friends are very grateful and I'm sure Lord Halkyn will also try and help when he returns from their tour."

The conversation was interrupted by the return of Alfred and Charles, and the bags were taken to the carriage. Alfred had seen Mrs Edwards on the way down the stairs and had explained that he would be visiting family. She did not seem pleased at losing her best tenant, but Alfred paid for the following few weeks rent, to try and console her, which did the trick and she had returned to her rooms happy. Alfred had not wanted her to see who was leaving his rooms, the less people who saw Laura the better.

The carriage set off, but it was only when the last street of London were passed that Alfred began to relax, feeling that the further behind London was, the safer Laura would be. The occupants of the carriage were quiet, each wrapped in their own thoughts about the coming weeks.

Each night they stopped at an inn, Martha and Laura shared a room, as did Alfred and Charles. Laura had felt bereft at being so far away from Alfred, but had scolded herself, he did not want to be near her. She found Martha's quiet confidence soothing and allowed the woman to take charge of everything. She had been embarrassed about money, but on the first evening Martha had put her worries at ease.

"Lord Dunham was sending Charles to Yorkshire anyway," Martha explained when Laura had offered to pay for her room. "There is some business to attend to involving the replacement of the steward of the property."

"But mine and Alfred's board is extra, you must let me pay for it," Laura insisted.

"Lord Dunham wouldn't hear of you paying, even if there was no cause for us to travel to Yorkshire. You helped Lady Halkyn. If there is an account to settle, I am sure Lord Halkyn would settle it. Do not worry, everything has been taken care of," Martha assured her.

As the days progressed, the travellers became weary of being stuck in a carriage for most of the hours of daylight, but Martha and Charles told Alfred and Laura about the estate to help familiarise them with the area they were going to be living in.

Eventually, the carriage turned into the parkland and Laura felt the first stirrings of excitement. This was to be her home for the next few months. Martha had explained that she was to live in the house as a guest until after the baby had arrived. Only then was she to think about what she needed to do, or where she wanted to live. Laura had never had a home and she was determined that she was going to enjoy every moment, however long it lasted.

The carriage stopped at the front door and the carriage steps were let down. Mr Smithson, the butler and Mr Lawson, the steward stood together, waiting to greet the occupants. Letters had been received from Lord Dunham giving instructions about the guests.

"Mr Smithson, how nice to see you again," Martha said, smiling at the butler. She had worked closely with him when her mistress had lived on the estate, when his quick thinking had helped to save his mistress.

"Miss Fairfield, welcome. I hope the journey wasn't too tedious?" the ever calm butler responded.

"Not too bad, although it is good to be on firm ground," Martha responded with a smile. "Mr Lawson, you are looking well, Lady Dunham sends her very best regards."

Mr Lawson, smiled and bowed slightly. He had worked for Lady Dunham's family for most of his life and was very fond of her Ladyship. The remainder of the party were introduced to each other and led inside.

Smithson led the guests to the drawing room, in which refreshments already awaited the arrivals. "Oh, lovely, a decent cup of tea," Martha said with feeling, moving across to start pouring. "Thank you Mr Smithson and these cakes look delicious, I see Cook is as efficient as ever."

Mr Smithson smiled slightly. "She is looking forward to the house being busy, the food for the staff doesn't stretch her talents enough," the butler explained the cook's frustration at producing far less fancy food when the family were not in residence.

Laura bit into one of the cakes and closed her eyes as the sponge almost melted in her mouth. She sighed when she finished the delicacy. "That has to be the nicest thing I have ever tasted," she said, her tone showing real appreciation.

Martha smiled, "Cook will be feeding you all sorts of delicious meals while you are here, she is wasted in a house that the family rarely visits now."

Alfred and Laura were shown to their separate rooms after they had had their fill of cake and tea. Martha and Charles had excused themselves, each having duties to undertake before the evening meal.

Laura waited until the door had been closed behind her and then turned slowly to take in every part of the room. This was not like one of Baron Kersal's barely furnished rooms, it had everything a luxurious bed chamber needed. A large four poster took centre place along the main wall. Facing was a glowing fire, with a chaise lounge and small table. A desk faced one of the two large windows that let the beautiful view into the room. The second window had a comfortable looking window seat, which was partially hidden behind a dressing table, set near the window for best use of the light. A door led into a small dressing room, containing washing stand, a fire place, and a screen which one could use when extra privacy was needed.

Laura sat on the window seat and through the window at the long drive. She must be in one of the principal rooms, as if she was a real guest. She had never met Lord and Lady Dunham, but she was inclined to think they had to be the kindest people who had ever lived.

She was disturbed by a gentle knock on the door. "Come in," she said and the door opened, and Martha entered the room.

"I hope you are settling in," Martha asked, looking around the bed chamber, checking to make sure everything was to her satisfaction. "Ah good, it is here." She moved across to a large trunk that had been placed at the foot of the bed. She opened the lid and began taking out dresses.

"Am I in the wrong room?" Laura asked, her heart sinking at the thought of being taken to a different room.

"No, not at all," Martha said with a smile. "Lady Dunham has recently given birth to a little girl and had the thought that these dresses may be of some use to you."

Laura flushed, she was well aware that her dress was little more than rags, since she had been forced to leave everything else that she owned behind in her room, once she had realised that she was being followed. Alfred would not hear of either of them approaching her lodging to retrieve any clothing or personal belongings. Added to that, she had travelled for days in the same dress. To say that it was travel stained was a huge understatement.

"I cannot accept those," she said quietly, noticing the shimmer of fabric she had only ever seen in a shop window, let alone touched.

"Do you not like them?" Martha asked, fully aware of how overwhelmed Laura must be feeling. "I believe one of the farmhand's wives is increasing, she may have a use of them, if you don't like them."

"Lady Dunham is giving them away?" Laura asked in disbelief.

"Yes, she doesn't like dresses at the best of times," Martha said obscurely, "but she especially didn't like the dresses she had to wear while she was increasing. She told me in no uncertain terms that she would be glad to see the back of them." Martha smiled at the recollection. She was sure that her mistress would soon need another new set of clothes, as she had the feeling that there would be a houseful of children at Dunham House within a few years, but for now Lady Dunham was refusing to accept just how quickly those babies would arrive.

Laura had moved slowly to the trunk, it was filled with every colour, and more types of material than she had ever seen. The quality of the dresses made her gulp, she would feel like an intruder wearing something so exquisite.

"They are beautiful," she whispered, reaching out to touch the material.

Martha smiled, "Yes they are. You are taller than Lady Dunham, but are smaller in the body than she is. I have extra lace and edgings that we can use on some of the dresses if we need to lengthen them. Would you like to try them on?"

"Yes please!" Laura said, her green eyes sparkling.

Chapter 10

That evening, as the four gathered together in the drawing room before eating, Alfred wondered what Gods had gathered together and decided that he deserved to be tortured. Laura had walked in wearing a dress that made her striking features stand out, and almost seem to hit him around the cheeks in an effort to say 'just in case you have not noticed how lovely she is, here is a reminder'. She had picked a deep emerald dress, which seemed to make her eyes almost leap out, they emphasised them so much. The deepness of the colour, tamed the rich red of her hair and she had tied it loosely at the top of her head, emphasising the slender whiteness of her neck.

He took a large gulp of his port, not only had the Gods made her with child, they made her even more beautiful and unreachable. His dreams would be tortured tonight.

A small table had been set up in the dining room, there were only the five of them, including Mr Lawson. Laura had taken to the elderly steward. His face was ruddy with spending so much of his time outdoors, and his thick grey hair was a little longer than was normally worn, giving him the appearance of being a little wild. His mannerisms and voice were so gentle and calming that within minutes Laura had fallen under his spell. He spoke very highly of Lady Dunham and chuckled as he reminisced with Martha about the days before Lady Dunham had married.

"Lady Dunham insists that I let her know if you are satisfied with the cottage that is yours when a replacement for you is found," Martha said to Mr Lawson.

"I am," came the firm response. "I am fond of my brother, but I could not face finishing my days in a city. I want to be able to roam the hills and torment the new steward," he chuckled.

The group laughed with him. "Is there anyone you know of who would like to take over the position?" Charles asked. Personal recommendation was always better than sending out an advertisement.

"Not really," Mr Lawson said with the first signs of a frown. "There isn't enough work here for a full-time steward. Since the major work has been done, the estate runs like a well oiled machine," he admitted. "If you attract a younger man, they are probably going to move on to a larger estate before too long."

"That's what I am afraid of," Charles admitted. "Lord Dunham is keen to avoid change after change happening. It can cause the rest of the staff to be unsettled and ultimately isn't good for the estate."

"I agree, it may be worthwhile looking for the older end of the workforce, someone like me, who wanted to slow down," Mr Lawson said, showing that he too had been pondering over the problem since he had decided that he wanted to retire.

"The only problem with that is less work and less hours, also means less money," Charles said with a small smile. "If there is a family attached with the steward that may not be an option that many can afford."

"Well I suppose all you can do is advertise for the post and see who comes forward," Mr Lawson said.

"Yes, I will send out an advertisement tomorrow. I think I will send it to the local papers in a wide area, to try and attract the most applications."

Mr Lawson turned to Laura and Alfred, "I'm sure Miss Fairfield and Mr Anderton have both explored this estate on previous visits, but I would suggest the walk to the top field is a good one. The views of the surrounding areas are worth seeing."

"It's my first time out of London, so every sight is worth seeing," Laura responded honestly.

"In that case, can I suggest a horse and carriage ride over the wider area?" Mr Lawson suggested, warming to the fact that he could suggest a whole range of places that the pair could visit.

Alfred listened in silence to the group. Charles and Laura seemed content to encourage the conversation along. Martha was a little quiet, but not as quiet as himself. He was a little out of his depth, as the countryside and all its ways were not his natural environment. Although he had been out of London before, he still considered himself very much a city dweller, even though it was the seedier side of the city.

The wine that he was drinking was easing the pain that he felt every time he looked at Laura, but it did cause him to agree to escort her around the estate the following morning, before realising what he had agreed to. The result being that he spent the remainder of the evening cursing himself for putting himself more in her company, when he should be avoiding her as much as he possibly could, for his own sanity.

*

Alfred awoke with a head that ached. Too much wine was never a good idea, especially when he had agreed on a horse and carriage ride. This would not be the comfortable carriage that they had travelled north in, but a practical one, which would emphasise, rather than soothe a headache.

Laura dressed in a simple brown dress. It showed just what a difference in quality she was used to, when an obvious day gown, felt like it was made from the most exquisite of material and trimmings. She hoped that she could keep the dresses after the birth of the baby, she would happily take them in and wear them until they dropped from her shoulders. Her previous dresses had been designed for practicality, whereas these were designed for elegance.

She sat next to Alfred on the double seat at the front of the carriage. It was the first time she had been close to him since they had left London, which felt like an eternity ago. They started off in silence, Alfred looking pale, with a deep frown on his forehead. Laura ignored the feelings that Alfred's silence brought and concentrated on looking around her. The open spaces felt a little daunting. In London everything was so close, noisy and confined, that it was strange to hear birdsong, and not be able to see another person for miles.

They had been travelling for about half an hour when Laura grabbed Alfred's arm. "Look, over there in that field! Is it a rabbit?"

Alfred followed Laura's pointing finger and nodded, "Yes, it is, although it's not staying around," he said as the rabbit disappeared into the hedgerow.

"That's the first time I've ever seen a live one," Laura said. "It wouldn't be alive long if it dared to venture along the streets of London."

"No," Alfred responded with a small smile, "Although I'm sure it wouldn't last long around here too, it's a popular dish."

"It must be fresher here though. Just imagine having fresh food all the time," Laura said with longing. Some of the food that was available in London was so old that very strong sauces had to be used to hide the rank taste. That was after getting rid of any live insects off it, of course.

"A nice thought, maybe there are advantages to being in the countryside after all," Alfred admitted.

The tension seemed to ease a little between the pair and they carried on in a more companionable silence, occasionally broken when one or the other saw something of interest.

They stopped at lunchtime, when Alfred saw a suitable spot near a small stream. He led the horse to the stream for a drink, before securing it to a tree and then set out the picnic that had been supplied by Cook.

"I will soon resemble the side of a cart if I continue to eat this much and do nothing," Laura said biting into a large piece of bread and cheese.

"You'll just have to stop being so lazy then," Alfred teased.

Laura smiled good-naturedly, "You are right, I'm just out of my usual setting a little and I'm not quite sure what I'm supposed to be doing. I have wanted to go into the kitchen and get Cook to put me to work!"

Alfred laughed, "I don't suppose many guests of Lord and Lady Dunham have done that before," he said.

"I expect not," Laura responded. "Do you know what I mean though, Alfred? This isn't our world is it? It's a dream, but one that will come to an end, and when it does the memory will keep me warm until my dying day."

Alfred heard and understood the wistfulness in Laura's voice. Their world was one that usually kept a firm grip of its occupants. "No, it isn't our world and I suppose longing for something that we can't have will do us no good." His words were not just referring to the gentle life, he longed for Laura far more than he longed for anything else.

"I suppose not," Laura said. "But I intend enjoying it while I can." She stretched out on the blanket that Alfred had laid on the ground and went to rest her head on his lap. She looked him full in the eyes when he looked as if he was going to move away. "I want a pillow, nothing else, are you going to be awkward?"

"No," Alfred said gruffly. Any contact with her was torture and he wanted to avoid it at all cost, but he was not a cruel man and she was having an enjoyable day which he did not want to spoil.

Laura lay her head on Alfred's lap and closed her eyes. She did not dare to keep them open, for fear they would betray the joy in finally being able to touch him, even though it was under duress on his part. She let the warmth of the day cover her like a blanket and relaxed into the ground.

Alfred studied Laura as she rested. She had a pretty face, spoiled by the grey pallor of her skin caused by a hard life and not enough fresh air. Although he did not want to alter the peaceful mood of the afternoon, he was curious to find out about Laura's background.

"What happened to your family?" he asked.

Laura covered her eyes, in order that she could open them. "Why?" she asked.

"I just wondered about them from something you said when Veronica had gone missing," Alfred explained.

Laura smiled, "Are Bow Street Runners never off duty?" she teased.

Alfred grimaced, "Probably not and it's Bow Street *Officers* if you don't mind, 'Runner' is a very insulting term," he said, reiterating the complaint of every Bow Street Officer who heard the nickname 'Runner'.

"Whatever you say Officer," Laura teased, but then put her hand down and closed her eyes once more. "I've no idea what happened to my family. I was brought up in a foundling hospital until I was sent out to work in a house when I'd turned eight."

"Were you a domestic servant?" Alfred asked.

"That's what I was supposed to be," Laura admitted. "Only I had the misfortune of being sent to a Baron's home, bet you can't guess which one?" she said with derision. "My hair colour attracted him, something out of the ordinary, you see. He was always looking to make as much money as he could."

"Surely he did not make you...." Alfred started. His blood boiling at the thought of an eight year old being forced into the life Laura led. He had unconsciously moved his hand to Laura's hair and started to stroke it comfortingly.

"No, he didn't, not then," Laura said quietly. "I was taken out of the scullery though, he didn't want me spoiling. I actually thought he was a guardian angel, rescuing me from the drudgery that was the scullery. Life in the foundling hospital hadn't been easy, but it nothing compared to the work I had to do once I was sent to the house. Some of the pans were nearly as big as me and woe betide me if I left any dirt on them. I was so

82

happy to be taken out of there. Unfortunately, it wasn't many years before I wished with my every fibre that he'd left me there."

Alfred kept stroking her hair. "When?" he asked.

"I was ten," Laura said, her voice flat. "He could get a lot of money for an innocent that young."

"He deserves to be hung," Alfred said angrily. He felt sick inside to think how many young girls suffered the same fate.

Laura was pleased at Alfred's response, but she did not let it show. "I've had a long time to realise that there was nothing to be gained in regretting what happened. I survived, I was fed and got paid, I may have hated it, but I didn't have many choices did I?"

"No, but who could do that to a child?" Alfred muttered darkly.

"Many people, which is why the Barons of this world get richer and get away with murder, literally. At least we have this to make up for it though," she said with a happy sigh.

"Yes, we do," Alfred said, stroking her hair. How could someone put an innocent child through such an experience? It was a miracle she had not turned into some bitter and twisted person, instead of the kind, considerate woman that she was. "Is that why you helped Lady Halkyn?"

"Maybe," Laura acknowledged. "I knew what was happening before he took Charlotte, and although I didn't agree with it, it didn't strike me about how wrong it was until I saw her face when she realised how she'd been tricked. She seemed too young and innocent to be forced into marriage with some old crony." Laura reflected on the part that she had been forced to play in the kidnapping of young girls, to force them into marriage with men who wanted a very young bride. Usually the type of men who could not get a wife through normal courtship.

"Yet, she was years older than you had been," Alfred pointed out.

"It still didn't mean it was right," Laura responded reasonably. "At least there were a few days before she was due to be married. Kersal had wanted to make sure she was under his roof before the gentleman came to collect his prize."

"I wondered why there had been a delay in taking her to the marriage ceremony," Alfred mused.

"He wanted to make sure any signs of a struggle had faded," Laura said. "Thankfully, Lord Halkyn visited two nights in succession, so she was able to seek his help. Luckily we picked the right man."

"Did you ever....?" Alfred asked. He had no right to ask the question, or to feel a knot in his stomach as he waited for the response.

"No," Laura said quietly. She moved and sat up facing Alfred. "Alfred....."

"It's none of my business, I'm sorry, I shouldn't have asked," he responded apologetically.

"You know what my job was," Laura said, with remorse. "I can't change my history Alfred, as much as I may wish."

"I know, I was being unfair," he said and he knew that he was, it was just when he had to imagine her with someone else, it did something to his insides that he was not able to stop. It was especially hard for a man like Alfred to deal with as he was usually so much in control.

"You couldn't be unfair if your life depended on it, you are too good," Laura said standing and shaking out her skirts.

"You know nothing about me," Alfred said, a touch bitter about the misplaced compliment.

"Well it isn't from want of trying," Laura said provocatively. "Now take me home."

Chapter 11

Each day Alfred and Laura either walked or rode out onto the land, both expressing a desire to see the extensive estate, which was partly true. They were both enjoying being out in the open after so much time spent indoors. Laura was enjoying noticing the different flowers and trees. She did not wish to appear ignorant, but felt comfortable enough in Alfred's company that she could exclaim in delight at each new sight.

The real reason though, was that they wanted to spend time together. They liked Martha and Charles and the evenings were spent with them and Mr Lawson, but during the day Martha and Charles had duties to perform. So, rather than spend time inside, under the scrutiny of the staff, they spent every moment they could outside.

Each day they talked, little by little getting to know one another. Laura was more forthcoming than Alfred about her opinions, while he tried to deflect away any talk about himself, but Laura persisted. They usually finished whatever walk or ride they went on with time spent near the stream that they had found on the first day. Laura usually relaxing on Alfred's lap, somehow this was the most comfortable for talking, each avoiding eye contact, which made it more anonymous in a way.

One afternoon, Laura decided that it was time that she found out more about Alfred. He had questioned her closely about her time in the foundling hospital and her life in London since the raid on Baron Kersal's house, but he had been more reluctant to offer information about himself.

She had settled into place on Alfred's lap and decided to try again. "So what attracted you to Bow Street?" she asked. "Do you like danger?"

"I don't think anyone likes danger, if they are honest," Alfred replied.

"I suppose not, but then what does attract you to a job that involves putting your own safety at risk?" she asked.

"It chose me, rather than the other way around," Alfred said, obscurely.

"That's sounds like an interesting story," Laura responded.

"Not really," came the response. "Why did you not come into the offices when you needed my help?" Alfred said, changing the subject as he always did when it seemed like the conversation was focusing too much on himself.

Laura moved quicker than most women in her condition could and sat up, facing Alfred. She put her arm over his legs and leant on the grass. "Alfred Peters, what are you hiding from me?" she demanded, sick of his aversion to speaking about himself.

"Nothing," Alfred responded, not meeting her gaze.

"Nothing, my foot!" Laura snorted. "How can you expect me to believe such a blatant lie when I'm used to dealing with some of the greatest liars and cheats that exist in society?"

"You really should keep better company," Alfred tried to joke.

"Ha, well I'm beginning to think that *you're* questionable company, you're being so secretive," Laura responded tartly. Her words had been said in jest, but the moment they were uttered, she knew she had hit a nerve with Alfred. His gaze caught hers for a second before looking away again, but in that second she had seen such a haunted expression that it made her ache inside. She suddenly realised that Alfred was right when he had said that he was not the person she had thought he was.

Laura waited for a few moments, wanting Alfred to speak first, but it was apparent that he was not going to. She reached over with her other hand and touched his cheek, brushing his face gently with the back of her fingers. "What is it Alfred?"

"You think I'm good and I'm decent and I'm anything but," came the quiet response.

Laura's heart skipped a beat, she had always been able to read people quickly and well, it had helped her to survive. It scared her to think that she may have been wrong with Alfred, but then she controlled her feelings, because he had never shown her anything but decency. "You have been good to me," she responded quietly, still stroking his face. "What happened that you think I would change my opinion of you?"

"It will," Alfred said dully. "But I can see that I am not going to get any peace until I tell you."

"You are right about that," Laura responded with a gentle smile. It worried her that Alfred looked so troubled.

He smiled, but it was a very small smile, before taking a breath and sighing. "I worked as an apprentice for a number of years. I was a clerk for a small business. I was like you, I'd been brought up in an orphanage, but I had a nicer place to go too."

"I'm glad," Laura said quietly, being able to picture the gangly boy that existed before the man emerged.

"I completed my apprenticeship, I really enjoyed the work. I like order and am methodical, I'm told," Alfred said with a smile at the compliment his employer used to tell him. "I worked there until I was nineteen and then things changed."

Alfred seemed to struggle with his memories, but for once Laura did not try to encourage him. She could see the torment on his face and waited patiently, her hand never losing contact with his cheek.

"My employer was a good man, he had a family, a wife and two daughters. Business had been quiet and I could see he was a little worried, but then things seemed to pick up. There was a difference though, in that the regular staff were kept well away from the new work. We were told that it was only the senior people that could be involved. It was his way of trying to protect us I suppose."

"It was illegal?" Laura asked, already guessing the answer.

"Yes, well paid, but illegal. It was something to do with forgery of documents," Alfred explained. "I still don't know fully what it was. Anyway, it appears Mr King, my employer, made a mistake on one of the documents and it was identified as a fake. It cost the men involved a lot of money and they weren't happy."

"What happened?" Laura asked, her heart pounding. Stories like this in her world, rarely had a happy ending.

"A fire occurred in the King household, which killed them all," Alfred said, struggling to keep control. "It wasn't an accident, the windows had been nailed down and a barricade put across the door. The magistrate said it was suicide, that Mr King's business was failing and he could not face the shame."

"Could it have been?" Laura asked.

"No!" Alfred almost shouted. "He adored his wife and daughters, they meant everything to him. If what they said was true and he could not face the shame, he would have ended his own life but not theirs!"

"I'm so sorry," Laura said, seeing immediately that the King family had replaced the family that Alfred had never had.

"I heard their screams, Laura," Alfred said quietly.

"Oh good grief, you were there?" Laura asked, horrified.

"Not at first," Alfred explained. "We had been given an evening out. It was money paid by the men involved to get rid of us until it was too late. I'd come back early, I don't know whether I felt that something was wrong, or what made me return, it wasn't usual for them to give us money, especially with them specifying that they wanted us to enjoy ourselves. So, I returned, but the fire was raging downstairs by the time I arrived, there were people there from the neighbouring buildings trying to get in, but there was nothing that could be done. I heard them screaming and then it went quiet."

Laura moved closer and wrapped her arms around Alfred, he was shaking at the memory. She held him close until he calmed. "What happened afterwards?" she asked gently.

"There was an inquest, but it was a farce and then that was it. They were going to let it all pass without doing anything. I couldn't allow that to happen. I wasn't going to let Mr King's kindness be repaid by my walking away and doing nothing about it," Alfred said, looking angry at the memory of how his employer had been let down by society.

"What did you do?" Laura knew that she held a decent man, every action and word he had uttered proved it to her, but she also knew what revenge could drive someone to and she worried about what he had done.

Alfred looked at Laura, before resting his forehead on hers. "I almost killed a man."

Laura stopped herself from the gasp that was in danger of escaping her lips. She must not react in such a way that Alfred would withdraw from her. She guessed correctly that this was the first time he had ever spoken about it to anyone. "Tell me," she whispered.

"You will leave afterwards in disgust," Alfred said quietly. He had tried to make his tone light, to appear that he did not care, but he did. His mind screamed at him not to tell her the rest, that he needed her to think well of him, but once he had started it seemed that he couldn't stop.

"I beg to differ," Laura said quietly, leaning closer and kissing him gently on the lips. "Tell me."

Alfred had not reacted outwardly to the kiss, but inwardly it had given him the confidence to continue. "I went into the offices, offering to pack everything up. I went through every piece of paper that was in that building. I was looking for clues, anything that would lead me to those involved. I found information, although it was well hidden," he admitted, "but I wasn't called methodical for nothing."

89

"It took months, I entered a world that I had never believed existed before," he said shaking his head slightly. "I didn't think I would survive, but somehow I managed. One by one I hit the people who were involved in the forgeries."

"Did you harm them?" Laura asked.

"Not initially," Alfred replied honestly. "I wasn't as hardened as I am today. I burnt down houses, offices and factories, making sure there was no one inside first. I thought it would help me feel better, that by getting my own revenge, I could finally put the Kings at rest."

"And did it help?"

Alfred smiled, but it was a bitter smile. "No, revenge doesn't, it just brings you down to the level of the person doing wrong doesn't it? I had become a criminal, just as they were. The reality was that they knew someone was onto them. It only delayed their business, they set it up again in different locations. One time though, I came across the main man, a really powerful, nasty and ruthless individual. He laughed in my face when I told him why I was doing what I'd done, and told me that business was not a place for sentiment."

"He'd fit in with some of the men I've met," Laura said with feeling.

"So, I pushed away my sentiment and gave him a beating he wouldn't forget in a hurry," Alfred continued.

"He deserved it," Laura said.

"Yes he did, but I'd become as bad as he was," Alfred said. "I didn't care what the outcome was as long as I achieved my aim. I wanted him to suffer and I wasn't prepared to stop. I'd lost my sense of right and wrong."

"But you did stop," Laura consoled.

Alfred stood up and walked a few steps away from Laura. "I was stopped, I was going to kill him," he said, turning his back to Laura. He could not face to see the rejection in her eyes.

"What stopped you?" Laura asked, her mind racing over the information she had been given.

"I didn't know at the time, but the Bow Street Officers were also onto the trail of the gang. They had been following me as well, I thought I was so good and yet I'd been followed for weeks. They knew exactly what I'd been doing. My now boss, Mr Frost was there. If he hadn't intervened, I would have killed a man that day and swung for it," Alfred said. He will never forget the expression in Mr Frost's eyes as he had spoken to Alfred.

Alfred had been held back by the Bow Street Officers and he had struggled, trying to finish the job he had started. Mr Frost had approached him and took hold of Alfred's shoulders. "My officers are going to let you go," he had said in his usual quiet voice. "You have two choices, finish the job you came here to do tonight and hang, or repay Mr King's faith in you and let this man go to trial and hang for his crimes. We have enough evidence, built up over months. I'm sorry it wasn't in time to save the King family, but we can only make choices about the future, we cannot influence the past. I can see the type of man you were and can be again. You have a choice to make about your future, but it's up to you, no one else can do it for you, it has been your crusade." He had stepped away from Alfred, and indicated that the officers should release the captive. Alfred had shaken himself in anger, ready to finish the task. Then he paused as the words sank in, and he looked at the Bow Street Officer. There was nothing but compassion in his eyes, he might not condone what Alfred wanted to do, but he understood. Alfred sighed, swinging for killing a man would not achieve anything, and he had relaxed slightly as the anger eased.

Mr Frost had seen the change as soon as it began, and indicated that his officers should make the arrest and take the offender away. Alfred watched the scene, almost dispassionately, it was as if he had not been a part of the evening. Mr Frost approached Alfred once the area was clear.

"You made the right decision tonight, young man," he said gently.

"I must be a coward," Alfred had responded bitterly.

"You are a bigger man for realising your action was wrong and responding to that. Don't ever consider yourself a coward. You did what was right, and that is harder than acting in the heat of the moment. What are you going to do now?"

"I don't know sir," Alfred had responded truthfully. He had been so focused on getting revenge that he had not considered his future at all.

"Come and see me tomorrow," Mr Frost had said. "We could use an officer like you."

"What, one who considers killing criminals?" Alfred had asked sarcastically.

"One who finds out the truth and works to bring the perpetrators to justice. I won't lie to you, there may come a time when you need to be able to kill, but we need people who won't give up when the job is difficult," Mr Frost had explained.

Alfred's life had changed from that moment. He had gone to visit Mr Frost and undergone training. He had repaid his employer's faith by being an efficient and diligent officer.

Laura interrupted Alfred's thoughts. "Well for whatever the reason was that you did, I'm certainly glad you stopped." Alfred would probably never know how heartfelt those words were.

"Just remember though Laura, that you are mistaken when you think I am a decent human being," Alfred said, still facing away from her.

Laura came around and stood in front of Alfred. "You reacted to your whole family being killed," she said, holding her hand up to stop Alfred interrupting. "They were your family in everything but name. You had been with them since you were a child. Of course you wanted revenge. It's to your credit."

"The ability to kill is never to anyone's credit," Alfred said.

"You have paid for your lapse," Laura insisted. "I'm not saying that you are an angel, anyone living and working in the areas that we know and live in could not survive if they were too good, but you are a decent human being, with principles and I for one am glad to know you."

Alfred was touched at her words. Only Mr Frost and Mr King had seen the potential in him previously, he was a little intense for most females that he had come across. The type of women who lived in his neighbourhood wanted a man who they were used to, worked, who got drunk, and had their fill of their woman when they wanted it. They did not want someone who believed and longed for a family and looked for ways to improve themselves. He shrugged his shoulders, outwardly trying to dismiss the compliment, but inwardly treasuring her words.

"Come on, let's return to the house," he said gruffly, but he offered his arm, an action he had previously refrained from doing. He had not wanted to cause speculation between the people they had just met. Laura's life was complicated enough, but today, after revealing what he had, he needed to feel close to her.

Chapter 12

Martha had noticed the relationship that existed between Laura and Alfred. She had wondered if they had known each other previously, or if the country air and the freedom they had was leading to deeper feelings developing. It was obvious that the three weeks which had passed had changed the pair. Both had gained colour, which was the result of spending much of their day outside, but their features had relaxed. Each looked younger as a consequence. Alfred smiled more than he had at the beginning and Martha noticed that he often looked at Laura with a kind of longing that she recognised; that of someone looking at something they could not have, but wanted it nonetheless.

Martha liked Laura, she was feisty and funny, but she was also warm hearted and a little bit vulnerable, especially about the impending birth. Ever practical Martha decided that it was time to start to make arrangements for the baby, which was reason why she had accompanied the party in the first place.

She entered Laura's bed chamber one afternoon when the weather had prevented Laura and Alfred venturing out on their daily excursions. Laura was sat on the chaise longue, with her feet up, reading a book.

"I've taken the liberty of ordering refreshments," Martha started. "I thought it would be good to have a chat without Alfred and Charles chipping in."

"That's nice, although I have never eaten as much as I have since I arrived here," Laura said, sitting in a more upright position and swinging her feet off the cushions, so Martha could sit down.

"You look all the better for it," Martha replied honestly. Laura's cheeks were fuller and her skin glowed, partly because of the sunshine and exercise she was getting, partly because of the good quality food. Her hair, never tightly restrained, glistened whenever the light caught it.

"That's a polite way of saying I have put on weight," Laura laughed. "I hope after the baby is born that all the weight disappears and I go back to how I felt before."

Martha waited until the refreshment tray had been delivered before responding. "I need to speak to you about the baby's arrival," she started gently.

"I keep trying to ignore it," Laura said with a groan. It was true, she was. As much as she had wanted this baby, after the last few weeks she had half regretted her actions. Her relationship with Alfred was such that she was sure that if she had not been pregnant, they would be more than the friends they were now. Although, she had to admit, it was only because of the baby that she had so much support. The result was that her emotions were constantly up and down, one moment happy with the way things were, one moment desperate for things to be different.

"Well from the looks of things, it won't be very long before you can't ignore it, whether you want to or not," Martha responded with a smile. "How long do you think you have left?"

"I know exactly. Six weeks," Laura said with authority.

Martha was surprised that Laura could be so definite. "Are you sure? Lady Dunham knew roughly, but could not be completely sure."

Laura smiled at the memory. "I know the exact date this happened," she said firmly. "My trade is such that babies can be prevented, they need to be, or we wouldn't be a lot of use for most of the time," she said in her matter of fact way.

Martha flushed a little in embarrassment, she obviously knew Laura's background, but speaking so openly about it, was embarrassing to someone who although older, was far more innocent. "I see," she replied.

"I've shocked you, I'm sorry," Laura said. "I shouldn't be so coarse."

"Don't be silly," Martha said, recollecting herself. "You should be exactly how you want to be, anything else would just make you miserable. I saw that when Lady Dunham had a season in London, it just wasn't her, and she was very unhappy. If you don't mind me asking, if you know how to prevent babies, why are you increasing now?"

Laura smiled sadly. "I am going to shock you again, Martha. I wanted this baby, so I purposely did not use the prevention methods I ought to have done. Go on, think badly of me, bringing a child into the world without any hope of support from the father."

"Did you love the father?" Martha asked, curious to find out the story behind the woman. It was obvious her pre-conceived ideas were wrong.

"Yes, and still do," Laura answered honestly. "I will do until my dying day, more fool me."

"Would he not support you, even if he was not in a position to marry you?" Martha asked.

Laura laughed, "Martha, you must believe these romance novels that the gentry read," she said, tapping her hand on the book on the table next to the chaise longue. "In real life women who work as I did never marry and have a family. Which man would want a wife with a background like mine?"

"But that shouldn't prevent him from supporting his child," Martha insisted, indignant for the unborn baby.

"He doesn't know about it," Laura said simply. "And if he did, he wouldn't believe that it was his. Alfred confirmed that would be the case, if I ever had any doubts."

"How so?" Martha asked.

"Alfred said that if he had been with a woman of the night, he would never believe that he was the father of her child, even if she later declared that he was," Laura said, a mixture of pain and sadness in her voice. She looked away from Martha, blinking back the moisture that had appeared in her eyes.

Martha frowned, it was a harsh response from the normally quiet, gentle Alfred. Perhaps she had been mistaken when she had thought he was so considerate. It seemed like an unusually unfeeling comment.

"So it is me and the baby," Laura said, rousing herself. "I don't intend going back to what I did before. I will hopefully get a position that accepts the child."

Martha did not know if Laura would ever find such a position. Most households did not want the encumbrance of children attached to staff, it was a diversion from work. She was hopeful though that Lord and Lady Halkyn would find something for her friend, Laura should not be left to fend for herself.

"Well we have to arrange with the local nurse to attend you at the appropriate time. I was there at Lady Dunham's confinement, but I'm no expert," Martha said.

"That makes two of us," Laura responded with a smile. "When do I need to make arrangements to leave after the birth?" She knew that she would have to make her own way and she needed to know when that would be.

"There is no hurry. We have no idea when Lord and Lady Halkyn will be returning to their property, and I would imagine they would want to see you, so there is no point making any plans at the moment," Martha assured her.

"You must want to return to your own position," Laura said. She knew that Martha had only travelled because of the need of a woman in the party.

"I was reluctant to come along, I admit," Martha said truthfully, "but Lord and Lady Dunham are on an extended visit to their family in London, so I may as well enjoy the change. I come from the north and although I am not from Yorkshire, it has so many similarities to my home that I feel as if I am returning to my homeland."

"Are your family still in the north?" Laura asked.

"One of my brothers is in the Navy," Martha said with pride. "The youngest boy has been apprenticed as a clerk in Liverpool and my eldest brother manages the family estate, although it is a lot smaller than it used to be." Martha was in touch with Thomas regularly, his letters keeping Martha up to date with local news. He had married a genteel lady, who had a small fortune, not enough to make the financial worries disappear completely, but enough to make him able to relax a little.

"Do you have any sisters?" Laura asked.

"Yes, one younger," Martha said. She was disappointed that her sister had never had the opportunity for a season, at least Martha had the one to look back on with happy memories. She loved to dance and very often imagined herself back in the local Assembly Rooms, taking part in a Cotillion or a Quadrille. "She is a governess to a local family, which is helpful to Thomas, as she can go home on her day off and help care for our mother." Poor Susan had been condemned to a life that had little hope of changing. If she was always caring for others, she would never have the opportunity to meet anyone who would consider marrying a girl without fortune.

"I never had a family," Laura said. "It must be nice to know that if you were ever in trouble, they would be there to help."

"It is," Martha responded. It was true that she loved and cherished her family, but how her life could have been different if only her father had not lived life to excess. "Although families can be a burden as well," she added thoughtfully. "Right, this isn't getting anything done, I shall leave you to your book and send a letter to the nurse, preparing her for our call when the time comes."

Martha stood up and left Laura's room. She returned to her own bed chamber pondering over what Laura had said. Perhaps the baby was a way of creating her own family? Although that brought its own problems in itself. She was thoughtful as she wrote the letter to the local nurse and sought Charles out to ensure it was sent out with the other letters of business.

A sort of truce had developed between Martha and Charles. Martha had wanted to maintain the level of animosity that existed between them when they resided at Dunham House, but she found that she could not in her current location. In Dunham House they were mainly apart, both having full jobs to attend to. In Yorkshire though, neither had as much of a demand on their time and so the contact between them was increased. Martha was not usually an antagonistic person, and she did not have the energy or the inclination to carry on a feud.

Charles had noticed the change in his opponent, but had not overly rejoiced in it. He was so afraid of relations returning to how they had been that he was usually on edge around Martha, in case he said, or did something wrong. He did not understand how he had got into this position, he was usually so competent in every aspect of his life, and admittedly he did not have much experience around women. He thought that the problem was that he had been attracted to Martha when he had first met her and had acted like a youth just out of the schoolroom. Instead of flattering her, like any man with sense would have done, he had insulted her. He had let his own insecurity influence his behaviour. His pleasure in shaking her composure was short lived, especially when the consequences were that she developed a real dislike of him. Inwardly, he kicked himself, every time she glowered at him, as only Martha Fairfield could do.

Although he was on edge being in Martha's company, Charles tried to encourage the contact between them both. He arranged for work to be carried out for which he needed the advice or counsel of Martha, just to have an excuse of spending time with her. He could not push her too far, but he was hoping that in time she would see him as a friend, if not more, rather than the ogre that had tormented her until now.

He asked her to go through the letters of application that he had received as a result of his advertisements for a steward. He could have asked Mr Lawson, and he would, but he valued Martha's opinion first.

Martha had been surprised at the request. She still stung when she thought about his interference with regards to the employment of a nanny, something that she had not managed to achieve before her trip. She sat in the study with Charles, reading through the letters carefully.

Charles watched the woman before him. The slight frown of concentration and the chewing of her bottom lip, signs of how deeply she was studying. Martha's absorption gave him time to dwell over the impact she had had on him. He had never presumed that he would find a life partner, working for a gentleman, a single gentleman, would not necessarily put ladies in his path and he had little enough time off to pursue them himself. So, he had resigned himself to the fact that he would remain unmarried. He was not too upset, he enjoyed his employment, liking his master and then his mistress, many men in his position did not have the freedom, or the close relationship that he enjoyed.

Martha Fairfield had disturbed him. She had come into his life, so calm and composed, always the voice of reason. She was handsome, rather than pretty, her features strong and plain, but not unattractive. It was as if her features expressed the inner person, calm, capable and no nonsense. She had rocked his composure and resurrected his insecurities.

So, for the first time in Charles' life, he had been interested in a woman. He had wanted to see what lay underneath that calm exterior and in his inexperienced befuddlement, he had gone about it in completely the wrong way. He had tried to antagonise her, not expecting the response he got. He should have known that the no-nonsense approach meant that she would deal with him in the same way, but he had also underestimated the way she had developed a dislike for him.

The top level of staff in any household usually worked together. They were in the position of being in the middle of the family of the house and the rest of the staff; not quite family, but not quite staff. A bond usually existed that made the in-between state more bearable, but because of Charles's foolishness, he had created a division.

Only once had she turned to him. When she had thought Lady Dunham was in danger, she had kept control until she had seen him and then had burst into tears. Charles had been shaken, her behaviour had been so out of the ordinary. He had asked her to trust in him and she had told him that she did, she had clung to him as if only he could rescue her. It had made him feel that he could achieve anything.

That had been the day, when everything was over, that he had realised that he was in love with Martha Fairfield. It was also the day that he realised how foolish he had been and how hopeless his case was. He had decided to try and help her, but the reality was that no matter how he tried, Martha misinterpreted his actions and the tension remained.

Martha stirred herself. "You obviously have your own opinions on these letters," she said a little stiffly, always wary that she would receive criticism from her comments. "But there doesn't appear to be anyone who would be suitable."

Charles smiled in encouragement, "That is what I thought, they are either applying for the job to gain a little experience and be off, or want it because they think it will be an easy role. I don't want to encourage someone who will ultimately neglect the estate."

"No, although Elizabeth will rarely visit now, this estate is very close to her heart, particularly because it was her first real home after her father's death," Martha agreed.

"I know, but that doesn't make these letters any more appealing," Charles said with a groan. "I suppose I need to widen the search, but that will take time."

"Are you looking to return to Lord Dunham soon?" Martha asked, surprised of the feeling that she did not want him to leave.

"I shall write to him. He did not specify how long he expected me to stay here, but it would be unreasonable to presume I could stay here indefinitely. We both will be needed at home at some point." He was careful not to sound as if he was making himself out to be more important.

"I know, Laura has said that she is to be confined in around six weeks, I wasn't expecting to be away for so long," Martha admitted.

"I suppose if I write and ask his Lordship for his advice, we can be guided by his response," Charles said with a shrug.

They were interrupted by Smithson, bringing in the post. Charles sorted through it and handed Martha a letter. "One for you," he said, leaning across to her.

Martha smiled, "It will be from Thomas, although he did write earlier in the week," she responded. Her letters from her brother were as regular as the sun rose every morning, the brother and sister may be hundreds of miles apart, but they were as close as ever.

She opened the letter and began to read, while Charles continued to open the other letters. Charles felt, rather than heard the change in Martha, her posture went stiff and the colour drained from her face.

"Martha?" he asked quietly.

It took Martha a few seconds before she realised that Charles had spoken. She looked at him, but did not really see him, or the concern on his face. She stood on shaky legs and turned to the door. "Please excuse me Charles, I need to attend to something in my bed chamber."

"Martha, is anything wrong? Can I help?" Charles asked, knowing full well that there was something very wrong.

"Oh no, no, just a letter," Martha said quietly, not turning to meet his gaze. "Please excuse me."

Chapter 13

Charles sat at the desk for some time, pondering about what to do. Martha had obviously received some news from home which had shaken her, but it was none of his business. He had offered to help and she had turned from him, he should just forget it and get on with his work, he argued with himself. He needed to send the letter to Lord Dunham after all.

He took out a piece of parchment and started to write. The introduction had barely been written, before he placed his quill on the ink stand and pushed back his chair with a sigh. She was upset, he could not leave her alone.

Martha heard the gentle knocking and knew who it was. She had sat at her dressing table with her money box set before her. It travelled everywhere with her, making her feel secure. Wherever she was, she had her retirement fund with her, no disaster would separate the two. Not until today, anyway.

She moved to the sofa placed at the bottom of the bed and sat on it, pretending to read the letter, but in her upset state, not realising that she still had some of the money grasped in her hand. The knock came again.

"Come in," she said, but her voice seemed unlike her own, detached almost.

Charles opened the door and walked into her bed chamber. A unique occurrence and not one that either would want becoming known by any other member of staff. Once Charles had stepped into the room he closed the door firmly behind him.

"Forgive my intruding Martha, but you were upset," he said walking across to her and sitting next to her without waiting for an invitation. "Something is amiss at your home? Are your family well?"

Martha looked at Charles, his brow was furrowed with nothing but concern, why would he be concerned when he did not like her? Her thoughts seemed to jumble as she tried to adjust herself to the change she was facing. "I…" she started, but then faltered.

Charles reached out and took her hand, then looked down in surprise at the money that she was gripping as if her life depended on it. He was certain that the money had not arrived in the letter, no money had fallen out when she had opened it. "Martha, tell me," he urged.

"Thomas writes, my brother….," she faltered again, before taking a steadying breath. "My youngest brother, has left his apprenticeship and joined a ship. He is currently somewhere between Liverpool and China. That is what Thomas thinks at any rate, he has made some enquiries at the dockside, but he cannot be totally sure. Young boys tend to look alike don't they?" Martha looked down at her hands. How long had it been since she had seen her brother, the baby of the family? In her memory he was still a little boy who was so sweet and obliging, how could he do something so foolish?

Charles squeezed her hands gently. "Surely it is not too bad? He is still in employment, he may make some money on the journey." Very often a portion of the ship's goods would be given to the sailors who had contributed to a safe, successful voyage, if he was lucky the boy may come back with a reasonable bounty.

"I-it's not that," Martha responded, regretting that she had opened the letter in front of Charles. She could not hide the real cause of her distress.

"Go on," Charles urged.

"The man who had agreed to the apprenticeship had not insisted on the payment up front, but is now demanding it, in addition to the money he has spent on my brother over the time he has been in his service. He is saying that it will cost him dearly because he has to start looking all over again for a replacement," she said, hanging her head with embarrassment at the poor behaviour of one of her relations.

Charles was well aware of the money that families had to pay in order that an apprenticeship take place, it was common practice. "Your elder brother must have known that he would have to pay at some point in the future," he said, still not understanding why Martha was so upset.

"Yes, but he has not got the money now. He says that although things are steady with the estate, what is left of it, mother has needed the apothecary many times recently and his reserves are depleted. He has no money to settle the account," Martha said.

"How much is he asking for from you?" Charles asked, realisation dawning on the request that the letter must contain.

"Two hundred pounds, or as near as I can give him," Martha said with a sob, saying the words out loud, making the reality of the request sink in and reducing her ability to hold back her emotions.

"Two hundred pounds!" Charles gasped. "Where on earth does he think that you could get that sort of money from?" That would be years of wages, even if she had spent nothing in the interim.

A laugh escaped Martha's lips, but it was a bitter one. "I had a legacy left me a few years ago and I saved half of it and I have been saving for my retirement since I started working. I had assured Thomas that I would not be a burden on him or on any of the others when I could no longer work. Thomas knows I have some money set aside."

"How much have you saved?" Charles asked, his heart sinking.

"Almost a hundred and fifty pounds," Martha acknowledged. "I am over thirty now, I was hoping that when the time came for me to leave Elizabeth I would not need to work for anyone else and could rent a cottage on the estate. Now it seems I will be working until my dying day. I will never save enough now. I would not have saved so much only for the legacy." The last words were finished with a sob and the tears that she had been fighting, finally came.

Charles reacted as he had the last time he had seen her cry and enveloped her in his arms. He cursed her brother for asking her to give up her legacy and savings. How could he ask a single woman to give away the only security she had?

Charles held Martha close and let her cry. He understood she was crying for more than her brother running away to sea and he did not condemn her for it. An unmarried woman had limited opportunities, a poor and aging one had even less.

As her sobs subsided, he gently rubbed her back, trying in his own way to soothe her. Eventually she stopped crying, but Charles continued to hold her. His feeling had gone from wanting to comfort her to something else, he was enjoying holding Martha in his arms and appreciating the feeling it gave him, as if she fitted perfectly.

Martha pulled away slightly, her cheeks were pink from crying and the fact that she had been leaning on Charles' chest, and although her cheek had been resting on his frock coat, she could still feel the movement of his body as he breathed. She had felt supported, comfort and security while being held, but it could not last, so she forced herself to move.

"I must send the money, there is no point in delaying," she said, her practical nature coming to the fore.

"Lord and Lady Dunham are not going to cast you off," Charles reassured her. "Look at the trouble they are taking for Mr Lawson."

"You are right, but I just wanted not to have to rely on someone else when the time came. Do you understand what I mean?" Martha asked.

"Yes, I do, but there are people who care about you and will want to help," Charles said, his arms had moved from her back to the top of her arms and he applied gentle pressure in reassurance. "Let me help."

"You?" Martha asked in surprise, pulling further away. "Why would you want to help?"

Charles panicked a little at Martha's movement. He was not ready to let her go just yet, he had no idea if he would ever hold her again. So he acted out of instinct rather than rational thought, and leaned in and kissed her.

Martha did not respond immediately, she was stunned, but Charles wrapped his arms around her once more and instead of resisting, as she should have done, she leant into him, wrapping her arms around his neck and kissed him back.

Charles had only needed a little encouragement to know that he had not made a mistake, Martha's reaction was beyond what he had hoped for and he groaned and pulled her closer. He could tell that she was unused to being kissed, but his was gentle and encouraging, pushing her a little every time she responded to him.

Martha's head was swimming. Only a few moments ago she had been crying, feeling desolate at her future, and now her heart was pounding as her mouth was being, teased and explored by Charles. She pulled at his hair, not caring if she was too rough and grasped his collar, dragging him closer, if it was possible. She became bolder when she realised that her actions caused him to moan and the kiss to increase in its intensity.

They stayed entwined until Charles leaned back further, he needed to feel her body against his. He pulled her across him as he lay back on the sofa, her skirts falling over his legs in a muslin curtain.

The action stirred Martha's senses, she was lying across a man, like some sort of wanton woman, she pulled away from him. "No," she said, hoarsely, breathing in large gasps of air to try and steady herself.

"Yes," Charles responded, his voice gruff, pulling her back towards him.

Martha put her hands against his chest and pushed him away, "No, this is wrong," she said firmly.

"It doesn't have to be," Charles said, sitting up, so he was closer to her. "Martha marry me, let me be the one to take care of you now and in the future. Marry me."

Martha stilled and looked at Charles, he looked as flushed as she felt and was breathing as deeply and erratically. "What did you say?" she asked, but her eyes narrowed with suspicion.

Charles saw the change and once again panicked. "I asked you to marry me, it would solve everything, I could look after you, you wouldn't need to worry about your future, I would take care of you," the ever calm Charles babbled like an idiot.

"But we dislike each other," Martha said, matter of fact.

Charles flopped back against the sofa, half in exasperation, half in defeat. "That wasn't a show of dislike," he said, referring to what had just happened.

"That was a heat of the moment lapse," Martha said standing. "I think it would be best if you leave now and we forget what has happened here today."

Charles stood, trying to keep his own emotions in place. He pulled down his waistcoat and frock coat and looked Martha fully in the face. "I meant every word and action that has happened today and I won't be forgetting it in a hurry. I am presuming this is a refusal, but if you change your mind, you know where to find me."

The door closed behind Charles before Martha could think of a suitable retort. She walked over to the desk and leaned on it for support, while she tried to calm her breathing. How had the day turned from being asked to give up her future and then offered an alternative, one that she had never allowed herself to dream of?

Married to Charles Anderton. Martha Anderton. The names suited one another. She shook herself, it was obviously said in the heat of the moment. He could never have seriously considered marriage to her, he disliked her, she disliked him. She closed her eyes in frustration, if she disliked him so much, why had she felt bereft once the feel of his lips on hers had faded? Why would the memory of that kiss haunt her every thought? She was a romantic fool and should know better.

Martha Fairfield looked at herself in the mirror and shook her head. She had come here to do a job and that is what she would do, the events of the morning would never be mentioned, or referred to, or thought of, again.

Chapter 14

Charles kept out of the way of Martha as much as was possible over the coming days, although he could not avoid her as much as he would have liked to have done. It stung. Her rejection had hurt him more than he would have ever predicted.

He prided himself on being sensible, calm, collected, and yet, whenever Martha Fairfield was in his presence, he seemed to turn into a gabbling fool. He had asked her to marry him. The problem was, rather than descending into panic when the realisation of what he had done had sunk in, and being relieved that she had all but laughed in his face, he was hurt. She was the only woman he had ever asked to marry him, or was likely to, and he had received a categorical rejection.

He was absolutely convinced that she liked him though. No one could respond to a kiss in such a passionate way and feel indifferent. The memory of her pulling his hair and tugging him towards her, he would not forget in a hurry. She had been inexperienced, but eager in the way she responded to his kiss. Somehow the fact that she was untouched by anyone, made him feel even more for her than he already did.

She obviously had some feelings for him, but she was so controlled, she had stopped things just when they were about to get interesting. He could still almost feel the material of her dress along his leg. If only he had not hurried her, of course she would pull away at that point. She was a genteel lady and he had moved things too fast. He had forgotten that she was of a higher class than him and he cursed himself. Of course she was better than him and he had tried to lower her to his level by dragging her onto the seat.

To be told that she disliked him after they had kissed, had stung his pride. How she could say something so cutting, when he had been barely able to breathe, never mind think, but she had brought him down to size. It was clear that although she was facing a future that was bleak, his proposal was repugnant to her. She obviously felt that he was no good for her. He would just have to be a man and treat her as coolly as she treated him, and if he could forget that kiss, he would be able to.

*

Martha was determined that there would be no opportunity for any more foolishness, but as time went on, she did start to feel guilty about her actions. Charles had treated her with nothing but concern and kindness, and she had been offensive. She inwardly cringed at the very thought of the way she had reacted. She had been brought up to behave with more consideration and respect for others, and was secretly ashamed of her behaviour.

Always the practical one, she decided that things had to be cleared between them and so waited until the bad weather had eased and Alfred and Laura had returned to their excursions outside. She did not want anyone to interrupt when she was begging forgiveness.

Charles looked surprised when Martha entered the study and closed the door. He did not have time to utter any sarcastic comment, as she approached the desk and stood before it, like a naughty school girl.

"I need to speak to you Charles, about last week," Martha started, not quite meeting his gaze.

"Which part of last week?" Charles asked, suppressing a smile, when his words caused a panicked glance, and then a flush in Martha's cheeks.

"I behaved rudely and in a manner that you didn't deserve. Your proposal was made out of kindness and I am ashamed that I responded so poorly," she replied.

"Have you reconsidered?" Charles asked, his voice expressing the surprise he felt, and much to his mortification, the hope.

Martha met his gaze, her expression showing the confusion she felt at his response. "No, I didn't take it seriously."

"I see," Charles responded, his face shuttered.

"I am sorry, I know you must detest me for how I have behaved and although I don't deserve your forgiveness, I hope that we can continue to rub along as we were prior to our silliness," Martha said quickly.

Charles seemed to sag at Martha's words. He looked at her and rubbed his hand through his hair, partly in frustration, partly to try and keep control of his temper. "Silliness Martha? I obviously don't know you at all, if you thought what we shared was nothing more than silliness."

Martha winced, she had practiced time and again how she would behave, how she would explain herself. She had even hoped that he would laugh about it and wave her embarrassment away, but standing in front of him was totally different to what she had imagined. He looked hurt at her words. She struggled with this, for she thought he had disliked her as much as she had disliked him. Well, perhaps she had not disliked so much as been annoyed at him, felt unsure around him.

Why this had happened she was struggling to understand. They had different roles within the house, there was no need for any antagonism to have developed. He was a handsome man and was charming, she had seen that so many times since she had met him. It was not disputed that the staff, Lord and Lady Dunham and anyone they came into contact, all liked Charles Anderton, everyone apart from herself.

Martha was a reasonable person, she had never made an enemy in her life, as far as she knew, but there was something about Charles that unsettled her. She had tossed and turned at night about it enough times before they had shared the kiss, but since then, she had barely had an hour's uninterrupted sleep. He had made her long for something that she had accepted was beyond her reach, and her insides were in constant turmoil because of it.

If she could have confided in someone, they would have said that she was a fool and told her to accept the marriage proposal. She knew that the marriage would give her everything she had wanted and needed, a husband, future security and maybe, if it was not too late, children of her own. So what was holding her back? She had no idea, just the uncomfortable feeling that he had asked her to marry him out of pity or on the spur of the moment and she felt that she could not accept a proposal on those terms.

Foolish, she most certainly was, but the only thing she had left was her pride and she could not sacrifice that for the security of a marriage. She was strong enough to sort this out, but Charles' reaction had confused her, and knocked her off balance. He seemed so upset at her words, and she had not expected that.

She tried to make light of it. "It was a moment of madness, surely you must see that?" She was struggling to find the right words, to make things as they were before she started worrying about the feelings of the man in front of her.

"Must I?" Charles said, "I remember being perfectly serious when I was kissing you. I could not have taken that lightly." He had moved around the desk until he was too close to Martha, unable to resist making her feel as uncomfortable as he was.

Martha took a step back, her heart beginning to pound. This was the moment she should leave the room, but instead she stood watching Charles as he matched her step away from him, with a step of his own. "Charles?" she asked nervously.

"Yes?" he replied. He did not want to kiss her. He was annoyed that she made him feel as if he meant nothing to her, when his dreams were haunted by her, but he could not help himself.

Martha stood still, her shoulders stiff, but she nibbled her lip, giving away the turmoil she was feeling. "We need to be civil to each other, while we are living under the same roof," she said, but the look in Charles' eyes was making her think that he was not actually hearing her words.

Charles reached out and stroked Martha's face, "I want to always live under the same roof as you," he said quietly.

Martha flushed, not sure whether it was his touch or his words that had affected her, but she stood motionless.

"Nothing to say, Martha?" Charles asked, continuing to stroke her cheek. "Are you not flattered that I want to live in the same home as you? That I want to be able to take care of you?"

Martha's mind was racing, this was not what she had been expecting, or anticipated. He was offering to look after her, she felt herself weaken and lean towards him slightly.

"Would you like that Martha?" Charles whispered, before leaning down and kissing her. He was gentle, certain that at any moment she would pull away from him, but she did not.

Martha's inner voice was telling her to move away, to push him away, but her body was telling her something completely different. She leaned into Charles and wrapped her arms around his neck, grasping at his hair. He was taller than her, and she had never felt that two people needed to fit together before now, but that was how she felt, as if they slotted together in perfect symmetry.

Charles welcomed Martha's movements with an appreciative groan. He pulled her closer and deepened the kiss. He was amused and aroused by the way she returned his kiss, she had obviously remembered everything they had done the first time. He nibbled along her jawline and down her neck, squeezing her when she arched her neck to allow him better access, moaning gently with pleasure.

God, she felt good and she was his. He returned to her lips, not wanting to leave them alone for long. This was what he had dreamed of, knowing what lay underneath that calm exterior. She was responsive and passionate and he wanted her.

His hands moved to her bottom and pulled her into him. He needed her to feel what effect she was having on him, but the movement caused a gasp. Martha pulled her hands from his hair and pushed him away slightly.

114

"Charles, I…." she said, breathless and flushed, but looking a little scared.

"Don't stop, please don't stop now," Charles said, aching for the contact to continue.

"What are we doing?" Martha asked, still using her hands against his chest to keep a barrier between them.

"Isn't that obvious?" Charles said, a little sharply. His emotions were screeching for release while at the same time his brain knew it was over.

Martha seemed to pull herself together at the tone of voice, or the words, Charles would never be sure which, but she moved away, completely out of his grasp. She did not bother to straighten her hair, or fix her dress, which had become disordered, but she stood straight and looked Charles in the eye.

"I can only apologise for my lapse, I did not wish for this to happen again," she lied, "and I can only assure you it will never happen again. I shall return to Dunham House if I have to, but we will not act so improperly again."

"Martha, don't be ridiculous!" Charles snapped. "We like one another, what is wrong with that?"

"Thank you for reminding me what a low opinion you have of me, yes I have been ridiculous," Martha said, somewhat unfairly. "I can only regret thinking that you were a better person than you actually are." She turned away and walked to the door. "I refuse to open myself to censure by the staff or my employers, so there will be no repeat of what has gone on today, that I promise."

Charles sank in the chair nearest the desk and groaned. What was it with this woman? One moment she was as cool as ice, the next she was acting like he was the answer to her dreams. He knew one thing though, she was the answer to his. He had never felt what he felt when he was touching her, and he was not going to stop trying to get through to her just how much they should be together.

For once in his life he was not going to be the dutiful employee. He was going to contact Lord Dunham and assure him that it was vital that both he and Miss Fairfield stayed exactly where they were for the foreseeable future. Return to Dunham House indeed! How could she think that, when there were definitely more kisses to enjoy here?

Chapter 15

Laura was feeling strange. She was restless and unsettled and she had no idea why. She had sorted out her room, much to the frustration of the maid that attended to the task every day, but she could not stop herself. She then started to walk through the house, picking up objects, gazing at them without seeing and then moving onto the next object.

Alfred had watched Laura from the top of the stairs as she had moved through the hallway. He smiled as he observed her, she was like a tight ball of energy, waiting to bounce away at any moment. The weather had been wetter in recent days, so he could understand her frustration, neither of them were used to doing nothing.

He walked down the stairs, his movement catching Laura's attention. Her smile lit up her face at seeing him, before it was replaced by a frown.

"I need to walk, or I think I will go insane," she said, with a scowl.

Alfred laughed, "Is that 'would you please accompany me on an excursion, Mr Peters?'" he teased.

Laura laughed, but tried to maintain the scowl, "Oh, gone all high and mighty have we? Fine, oh great one, May I trouble you to accompany me on a walk?"

"Of course," Alfred smiled and offered his arm.

They strolled through the formal gardens before reaching the border of the wider land. Laura examined the flowers as they walked. "It must be wonderful to have not to worry about the future, to just have a life where you can enjoy the flowers," she said a little wistfully.

"I'm sure Lord and Lady Dunham have worries, just different ones to those which will trouble people like us," Alfred said, remembering the all too real worries that they had faced not so very long ago.

"I suppose so," Laura replied unconvinced.

"Are you jealous?" Alfred asked, partly teasing, partly curious at Laura's apparent envious streak. He had not noticed that about her before.

Laura was soon to reassure Alfred with her response. "Jealous? No!" she exclaimed. "I would just like to know what is going to happen in the future, I suppose. Don't mind me, I've had too much time on my hands and am restless."

"I can understand that," Alfred agreed. "Don't worry about the future, I think it will work out fine once Lord and Lady Halkyn return."

"We don't know when that will be," Laura said.

"I would have thought it would have been before now," Alfred responded with a frown. "Lord Halkyn was not funning when he said that he was going to show his bride the world. I wonder where they went?"

Laura looked at Alfred sharply, before managing to school her features. "Do you need them to return, do you need to leave?" Her heart rate increased in dread of his response, she had come to rely on him so much over the previous weeks. His leaving was her biggest fear.

"I was given unspecified leave of absence," Alfred responded. "I should let Mr Frost know that it is going to be longer than anticipated, it is only decent. He has been reasonable with me, it is only fair that I should keep him informed."

The response was not quite as reassuring as Laura had hoped, but she could ask for no more. Alfred had a job in the city, which he took seriously and the fact was that she could never return to London, it would always be too much of a risk for her. So, even if her wildest dreams were realised and Alfred fell madly in love with her, they could never be together. She walked on with a feeling of lead in her stomach. She would have to become accustomed to life without him.

They reached a bench on the very edge of the formal area. It was placed to enable those who did not want to walk further into the fields to sit and admire the wider land. Laura paused as they were passing the bench.

"Would you mind if we rested for a while?" she asked.

"Not at all, are you well?" Alfred asked, immediately concerned at Laura's pale face.

"I'm fine," Laura replied, with a thin smile, but she sank into the bench as if it was the most comfortable chair she had ever sat on. "I think a few moments here, before we continue and I will be fine again." She could never explain to him that every time she thought of him leaving, she felt sick to her stomach. Especially so today, with his talk of Lord and Lady Halkyn's return, and contacting Mr Frost. She needed a few moments to gather herself.

They sat in companionable silence for a few moments, each enjoying the other's company. Alfred broke the silence eventually.

"I never thought that I would get used to seeing so few people. London is so busy that I never felt totally alone, but here, there is no one for miles, and yet it is a comfortable feeling," he said quietly.

"Apart from me, sitting inches away of course," Laura replied with an arched eyebrow.

Alfred gently pushed her shoulder, "You know what I meant, you picky woman!"

Laura smiled, "I did, it's just that I get worried when you go all melancholy on me."

"Never that, with you around," Alfred said good-naturedly. "I never thought I'd like the space, I suppose I never even thought I would see it, but I find it beautiful."

"I really do know what you mean," Laura said seriously. "We are all so wrapped up in trying to make a living in London, that we don't have the time or the money to venture into the countryside."

"I don't want this to be the only time that I ever see it," Alfred said, half to himself.

"Promise you will visit me," Laura responded, urgency in her voice.

"What?" Alfred asked, surprised at the change of tone.

"Promise that you will come and visit me," Laura repeated. "Alfred, I need to know that I will see you again." Gone was the reserved Laura, she needed to speak to him now, in case their time was limited.

"Laura, I can't offer…" Alfred started, waving his hands in Laura's general direction.

Laura's blood began to boil, he was so honourable but yet he could not see what was right in front of his face, that they were meant to be together. "Am I asking for anything other than a visit? I think you will find Alfred Peters, that I am not," she responded offended.

"I just didn't want you to think I was promising anything if I agreed to visit," Alfred said, floundering a little at the anger pulsing from Laura's every pore.

"Don't flatter yourself," Laura snapped, anger making her speech more careless. "You've made it quite clear that you find me repulsive!"

"That is not true!" Alfred snapped back. "How could you say that I find you repulsive when we had the night that we shared?"

"But now I'm with child, you do," Laura responded, standing and folding her arms.

"You are carrying another man's child, do you want me to rejoice over that?" Alfred snapped, standing to face Laura. "What do you think I felt when I saw you, no, felt that you were with child that evening when you followed me home?"

Laura's anger was reduced slightly at the look of pain in Alfred's eyes. "I would have expected you to have asked me civil questions instead of jumping to your own conclusions and condemning me," she said in a quieter manner than her last outburst.

Alfred sighed, "I know your background Laura, I don't think my conclusions were unreasonable were they?"

Alfred's words incensed Laura, tears of anger and frustration sprang to her eyes. She put her hands on her hips, squeezing herself tightly, to prevent reaching out and strangling Alfred. "You fool!" she spat. "All the signs have been there before your bloody eyes and you've ignored every one of them! You're the father of this child and you damn well know it! Add up the dates Alfred! You ought to be ashamed that so far, you are proving to be the worst of fathers!"

Alfred paled at the words. He had felt anger in his life, but never since the death of Mr King and his family had he felt such blazing fury. "How dare you level such an accusation at me?" he snarled at Laura, his anger barely contained. "I would have thought better of you Laura, than trying to blame your folly on a decent man, and yes, even after all that has happened, I class myself as a decent man. Don't ever mention this to me in the future, or you will never see me again, I promise you that."

When Alfred had finished speaking, he turned and walked away from Laura, his fists in tight balls at his sides. He needed to escape. Laura knew him, they had been so close over the weeks they had been together, he had thought her the person who knew him most in the world and thought highly of him. He had thought highly of her, had loved her, he supposed, or as close has he had ever got to loving anyone.

How could she have said those things? Why now? Did she think that he was now so deeply involved that he would throw up his hands in surrender and accept what she was saying? If that was the case, she did not know him after all. He would never be forced into a situation which he did not want.

Alfred stormed across the fields, steam almost coming out of his nostrils as he walked. The lack of people today was an advantage, as Alfred was sure that he would kill the first person that said a wrong word to him. Laura had hit on his deepest desire, and it hurt that she had hit it dead centre.

He longed for a family. The likelihood of him having one was slim at best, as he would never put his wife in the position of being a young widow and in his line of work that was a real possibility. So, he had avoided all contact with marriageable ladies. With his background, first hunting down Mr King's killers, and then working as a Bow Street Officer, it did not really need much effort to avoid women, he worked more than he played. It did not take away the fact that he wanted to be a husband and father though, since he wanted to give a young life the secure upbringing that he had not experienced.

Laura's accusation had shaken him to the core. If he *was* the father of her child, the thought was terrifying. He would have brought a child into the world in the worse possible way, to an insecure future. He felt sick at the thought.

As he walked he calmed a little, Laura was angry, she had spoken out to hurt. Although she had succeeded, Alfred became more magnanimous. She was a woman in an uncertain position, and of course she would try to secure her future and that of her baby. He just wished that she had chosen a better solution. He did wonder about the night they had spent together, but dismissed it. He was sure he was not the father, and that Laura was just lashing out.

*

Laura sank onto the bench after Alfred had stormed off and dissolved into tears. If she had been able to think coherently, she would probably have laughed at herself. The last time she had cried was the day that she had realised that Baron Kersal was not her saviour, after the man who had taken away her innocence had dressed, thrown a few coins on the bed and had left the room. Her tears then had been of fear and shame, her tears now were of the same.

How could she have lost her temper so foolishly? Alfred had told her that he would not believe it if a woman of the night told him that he was the father of her child, and yet here she was, shouting that very thing at him, in the worst possible way. He would probably never speak to her again, in fact if he stayed it would be a miracle. He would see it her story as a poor way of repaying all his kindnesses.

Laura was at a loss. He would never believe her. She had condemned her unborn child to never being accepted by its father and she had no idea how to resolve the situation. She had always been capable, able to keep herself contained to deal with what life threw at her, but this was beyond her. She had created a life knowingly and she had not thought through the reality of it.

In her heart, she supposed that she had hoped he would guess and accept her and the baby and they would live happily ever after.

Laura dried her eyes roughly, angry with herself. She was not one for happily ever after! That only happened in fairy stories that children were fooled with. She had to face reality, this child was going to be brought up by one parent and there was one thing she could be certain about, the child would be sure of its happy ever after, because she was determined to break the cycle. She would do everything in her power to make sure that her baby would have the chances that she herself had not.

Laura stood and squared her shoulders, she could do this, she was strong enough. Suddenly, she doubled over in pain and groaned. As the pain eased, her breathing slowed a little, but her heart still pounded, there was something wrong with the baby. All her fine thoughts and promises and already she was in a situation where she could do nothing, this was too early.

She gripped the bench and tried to stand, and when the pain did not return, she tentatively began to walk towards the house.

Never had such a relatively short walk taken so long. Laura would walk until the pain washed over her and then sink to her knees, unable to do anything, but gasp. Once the pain subsided, she would push herself off her knees and walk, hunched over, through the gardens.

It was only when she reached the rose garden that she saw an undergardener and managed to call him over, through gritted teeth.

"Yes, Miss?" the young boy said, approaching her with caution.

"Get Miss Fairfield, tell her it's the baby," Laura gasped, the pain washing over her once more.

"Yes Miss!" came the response, as he turned and ran towards the house.

Laura remained in the position she was, since somehow asking for help had drained some of her resources and she had not the strength to move. It was taking everything she had to concentrate on breathing. It felt like hours before she saw the welcome figures of Charles and Martha running over the lawned area, with the under gardener leading the way. They all arrived breathless, but Martha crouched down in front of Laura.

"Laura, what's wrong?" she asked, feeling Laura's heated forehead with her hand.

"The baby...," Laura gasped, "But it's too early, it's three weeks too early," she sobbed.

"They come when they're ready," Martha said, in her calm matter-of-fact way. She stood immediately and moved to Laura's side. "Charles, we need to get her to her bed chamber immediately. Benjamin, tell Mr Smithson, we need the midwife for Miss Atkinson."

Benjamin ran off again immediately, his eyes round with the excitement of the day, while Charles took Laura's other side. Together the pair lifted Laura and half supported her, half dragged her back to the house.

Laura kept muttering as they walked, all that was coherent was "The baby."

As Martha walked, she reassured Laura. "Don't worry, Lady Dunham's baby arrived early and she was fine. They have their own time, don't worry, we will soon have you inside." Martha kept her voice level and soothing, she was fully aware that Laura was frightened, just as Lady Dunham had been.

Laura was led into the hallway of the house and visibly relaxed. So much had been running through her mind, one thing being that she might have the child out of doors. Once inside, she knew it would not be long before she was safe in her bedchamber.

Smithson, hovered near the doorway, offering to take over from Martha, in supporting Laura. Martha moved to allow the butler to help, but Laura protested.

"No," she gasped, gripping tight to Martha's arm. "He needs to find Alfred. I need Alfred."

There was no surprise betrayed by the two gentlemen in the hallway. Martha accepted Laura's words, but instead of turning to Smithson, she turned to Charles.

"Charles, Mr Smithson can help me with Laura. Please find Alfred, he left the house with Laura, so I am presuming that he is still outside," Martha said calmly.

"He was angry," Laura gasped.

"Shh, don't worry, he will soon be found." Martha soothed, not wanting Laura to air her troubles in public.

Charles nodded and left the room, while Laura was carefully, but firmly helped to her room. Charles walked to the stables, if Alfred had gone off in a temper, it was likely he would not be in the formal gardens. Alfred in a temper, Charles mused as he walked. What complicated lives the temporary residents of Home Farm seemed to lead. The ever calm Alfred losing his temper he could barely imagine, but whatever had happened, it was obviously important to Laura that he return.

Chapter 16

Alfred paced the dining room for the thousandth time. "How long do these things take?" he demanded of Charles, who was sat trying to offer comfort in his own quiet way.

"I've little more experience than you, I'm afraid," Charles said apologetically. "I don't think one can tell how long it will be."

"But it's been hours!" Alfred said, once again walking towards the window, resting his hand on the frame, before turning back and walking to the fireplace and then to the dining room door.

Charles watched the young man before him. He was acting almost identically to the way Lord Dunham had behaved when his wife had been giving birth. It was obvious that Alfred and Laura had feelings for each other, a blind man could have seen the regard they shared, but he wondered about the child. Charles shook himself, it was not his business to wonder and if Martha was in the same position, he would like as not be acting in the same way. The thought of Martha being heavy with another man's child was enough to stop Charles dwelling and scowl into the fire.

The door opened and both men spun their heads, expecting to see Martha in the doorway. Instead Smithson entered, "Mr Anderton, Mr Peters, Lord and Lady Halkyn have arrived."

The newcomers entered the room, looking like the newlyweds they were. Happiness seemed to glow around them and they held each other's arm, as if they could not bear to let go of one another. Their blonde heads leaning towards each other, not quite ready to allow the rest of the world into the one they had created.

"Lord Halkyn," Charles said, bowing to the Lord and Lady. "We were not expecting you."

"No, we only returned to London a sen'night ago. Walter told us about your visit Mr Peters, and there was a letter waiting for me from Dunham, gloating that he had helped because of my dallying on our wedding tour. Lady Halkyn insisted we leave the following morning," Lord Halkyn replied, with an indulgent look at his bride.

"I needed to make sure Laura was well," Lady Halkyn explained, a flush on her cheeks. She was a beautiful young woman, and at first glance it would be presumed that her looks had attracted Lord Halkyn, when in reality it had been her spirit and vulnerability. "Where is she?"

"Ah, she's a little unavailable at the moment," Charles said, himself a little embarrassed, not used to talking of such things with a young lady.

"She is well?" Lady Halkyn asked, alarmed.

"She is currently delivering her baby and it is taking an age!" Alfred said through gritted teeth.

Lord Halkyn looked with surprise at the Bow Street Officer, but his attention was soon taken by his wife.

"With child? Oh my goodness me!" Lady Halkyn exclaimed. "I must go to her."

"Charlotte, I don't think…." Lord Halkyn started, ever the one wanting to protect his wife from anything he thought she would find distasteful.

"Don't worry," Charlotte smiled at her husband. "I shall be fine."

Charlotte left the room, to be guided to Laura's bed chamber by Smithson. Lord Halkyn turned to Alfred. "Right Peters, you had better tell me what's been going on. I leave you alone for five minutes, and you've obviously gone and got yourself into all kinds of trouble!"

*

Laura had never been so relieved that an event was over in her life, when she was finally handed the swaddled bundle that contained her daughter. The midwife remained until she was satisfied that everything was in order and then left, informing Martha and Lady Halkyn that she would visit on the morrow.

Laura was aware of conversations going on around her, but had no comprehension of their content. She was too engrossed in staring at her baby, her own child. The baby looked back at its mother, with a stare that seemed clear, before falling contentedly asleep, seemingly happy with her lot in life. Laura gently stroked the side of her face, marvelling in the softness of the skin and the feel of downy hair.

She looked up as the door opened, to realise that Charlotte was leaving the room and turned to Martha in question.

"Don't worry, she is only going to tell the gentlemen that mother and baby are well. She shall return shortly. I expect you'll have a lot to talk about," Martha said quietly, finishing off fixing the bed cover over the new mother.

"We will," Laura agreed. "I am so glad this is all over," she sighed and leaned back into the pillows. "I thought she would not survive being early. I have never felt such panic when the pains started and I realised what was happening."

"Well she looks strong enough to me," Martha said with a smile, leaning over to the child. "She is beautiful, have you thought of a name?"

"Frederica," Laura said, not quite meeting Martha's gaze.

"That is a lovely name," Martha said gently. "A variation of her father's name that will suit her, I'm sure."

Laura looked horrified at Martha, before her eyes filled with tears for the second time in a day. "You know?" she whispered.

"I guessed," Martha said. "I recognise the looks you give each other and when you said that you were sure when it had happened, I obviously don't know, but I had a suspicion that it was tied in with Alfred somehow. Does he know?"

"I told him today," Laura said with a sob. "I shouted it at him," she said with a half attempt at a laugh, which turned into a hiccup. "He won't ever believe me."

"Give him time," Martha said reassuringly.

"No, he will never believe me," Laura said with conviction. "And if I'm being honest, I can't blame him. I'm not sure I'd believe me if I were in his position."

Laura would have taken comfort if she had known the way that Alfred had reacted during her labour and when he had been told of the safe arrival. He had sunk into a chair and only when he had been handed a large glass of brandy had he been able to recollect himself enough to join in the conversation that was going on around him.

*

During the first week after Laura's confinement, Alfred felt as if he had lost something. He had told Lord Halkyn everything that had happened to bring him to Home Farm and Lord Halkyn had assured him, in his own direct way that Laura was now his responsibility and he would make sure that she was settled somewhere safe and would be looked after. Alfred should have felt relief, and he did for Laura's sake, but it also left him feeling hollow inside. He could not scrutinise his feelings as to why, he just acknowledged that he felt lost.

He wrote to Mr Frost and informed him of the developments. He thought it only fair to let his employer know what was happening. He also asked when he would be expected to return. For some reason, the thought of returning to his old life was no longer as appealing. He dreaded receiving the letter he would likely soon receive from Mr Frost, with instructions on when he would be due back. There was nothing he could do about it, because he felt that it was his livelihood and something that he was good at, but he had seen something different and it had unsettled him and made him want more.

It would also mean leaving Laura and the baby and he was not happy about that either. Laura was the only person that he had any real feelings for and the thought of never seeing her again, made him feel sick. Laura had tried to get him to promise that they would stay in touch, but the reality was, that once he had returned to London and she had gone goodness knows where, they would probably never see each other again. Work and cost would prevent them, they did not have the freedom that a genteel person had.

The baby. That was another issue. He knew Laura did not lie, especially to him, they may have only known each other a short time, but they had confided everything to each other. He trusted her and yet her announcement had seemed so out of character. He had not believed her, he had been so angry with himself and her, but then, in the depths of the night, he had wondered if it could be true. He would toss and turn and then get angry with himself for believing something that was obviously not true, and continue to torture himself until falling into a disturbed sleep.

It was these unsettling thoughts that took him to Laura's bed chamber one morning. Lord and Lady Halkyn had not risen, and Charles and Martha were busy with their own duties. Alfred had waited until the maid had been in the room and then knocked quietly on the door. He heard Laura's muffled voice and opened the door.

Alfred paused when he saw the look of surprise on Laura's face. "Alfred?" she asked in wonder, never having expected to see him again, let alone in her bed chamber.

"I wanted to see how you were," Alfred said gruffly, embarrassed now that he had done it, knowing clearly how inappropriate it was to enter a woman's bed chamber, let alone one who was confined.

"Well you'd better come in then," Laura responded, hiding the surprise and delight at seeing him. She knew she would have to tread carefully if not to cause another argument.

Alfred entered, and closed the door behind him. "I can't stay long," he said.

"That's fine, it's just good to see another face," Laura said with a smile. "Charlotte and Martha are really kind, but unfortunately they can't stay all day."

"Are you being demanding?" Alfred asked with a grin, relaxing immediately with her.

"Of course," Laura responded, "Would you expect anything else?"

"No," Alfred admitted, sitting on a chair next to the bed. "How are you?"

"Bored," Laura said with a groan. "They tell me I have to stay here another week, but I think I will go insane before then," she explained.

"Like the outdoors now, do you? I thought we'd never get the city dweller out of you," Alfred teased.

"I hate being inside, just as much as you," Laura responded tartly, but then became serious. "I've missed our walks most of all."

"I have too," Alfred said honestly. "I am sorry for storming off and leaving you, if I'd have known the baby was going to arrive....." he apologised.

"I know, you would never have left me," Laura reassured him. "I didn't realise it myself until you were no longer in sight."

"It's probably because of me that she came early," Alfred said. That thought had haunted him, if anything would have happened to the baby, he was not sure he could have ever forgiven himself.

Laura reached over and took his hand, squeezing it. "As Martha said, they come when they are ready. I don't think you had any effect one way or another. I am sorry we argued though," she said, holding fast onto the rough hand, that she wanted to kiss, but could not for fear of him pulling away again.

"I am too," Alfred acknowledged. "What you said…."

"Don't let's talk about it now," Laura said. "I want to spend time with you were I am not afraid to say anything for fear you will walk away again. We have time in the future to talk about what I said," she could not risk him withdrawing from her again, he meant too much. She had pushed him too quickly, too far, and now she must take things slowly and tell him the truth a little at a time.

"Are you sure?" Alfred said, feeling relieved and disappointed at the same time.

"Yes, I want to hear what has been going on while I've been missing," Laura said, smiling.

They talked until Alfred decided that it was time he left. He had stayed for over an hour, far longer than he had anticipated, or Laura had hoped for. Throughout the whole time, Laura had kept hold of his hand and Alfred only pulled it away, after he had placed a kiss on her fingers.

"Go to sleep," he instructed. "I can see I have tired you, rest now."

"Yes, master," Laura teased, but she snuggled into the pillows and pulled the cover up. "Will you return?"

"Yes, I shall see you tomorrow," Alfred said, before leaving Laura to dream of houses in the country with Alfred and Frederica waving at her from the window.

Chapter 17

Charles was frustrated. He was not an unfeeling man and the arrival of Lord and Lady Halkyn meant that Laura would receive the support she deserved and which they all had been waiting for, but unfortunately for him, it meant more work. He did not mind that in principle, in fact it had been more like a holiday than work over the past few weeks, but more tasks to do in a day meant less time with Martha Fairfield, and that frustrated him.

He had planned to kiss her at every opportunity that presented itself, only with Lord and Lady Halkyn in the house, those opportunities were none existent. Martha spent her time between Lady Halkyn and Laura who was still confined and he spent his time with Lord Halkyn and Alfred. Only at the evening meal did they meet.

Martha looked more in control than ever. Charles could tell that she was more at ease now that there was no reason that she would find herself alone with him again. If he was a true gentleman he would leave her be and forget about her and what she meant to him, but in this matter he was not a gentleman, he was a man of business and he ached for Martha Fairfield.

Lord Halkyn had decided that Laura should stay in the area. That way, she would always have the support of Lord Dunham if she needed it. He had also decided in a name change.

"She should adopt Mrs Atkinson," Lord Halkyn said to Alfred and Charles one morning. "It will help create a background for her, a young widow moving to the north, to escape her grief."

"What about the staff here?" Alfred asked, not willing to examine why he did not like the term, Mrs attached to Laura's name.

"They are loyal to the Dunham's," Lord Halkyn said, "that was proven time and again when Elizabeth stayed here. There will be no issue with them."

"She will need a job," Charles said, "But she will struggle with the child."

"She has told Charlotte she has some money set aside and I will provide her with an income, she won't need to work if she chooses not to," Lord Halkyn said.

"It is not your responsibility to look after her," Alfred said, a little defensively.

Lord Halkyn, looked assessingly at the young man before him. He had always considered Alfred older than himself, when he had dealt with him previously, but he looked a lot younger now. He no longer bent slightly as he moved, almost as if he was ashamed of his height. He had filled out and was a healthy colour, hardly recognisable as the thin, drawn officer, who had attended his residence all those months ago.

Lord Halkyn had some sympathy with the young man, but he was also a man who was not used to indulging others, not until he had met his wife, at least. "And if not mine, whose is it?" he asked, with the raise of an eyebrow. "She saved my wife from goodness knows what, and directed her to me, and I shall be grateful to her until my dying day. So, yes, I do feel some responsibility for her, unless of course, you want to take over the role."

Alfred glowered at Lord Halkyn's mocking tone, which only amused the aristocrat even further. "I cannot support her, as you damn well know."

Lord Halkyn laughed, "Well you could, but you obviously aren't prepared to, more fool you, so I shall continue with my plans." Lord Halkyn turned to Charles. "Please find a small cottage near here that would be suitable. I shall leave it to you to secure it. No doubt once it is secured my wife and Miss Fairfield will want to take a part in its furnishing, so just keep me informed and send me the bills," he said dismissively.

Lord Halkyn left the room and the two men stared at the door for a moment in silence.

"I thought Lord Dunham was straight to the point," Charles said, ruefully, trying to break the atmosphere.

"If I didn't know that he was a decent man, I *swear* I would have to kill him," Alfred ground out.

"That's what I'd have said too, and I realise that we say this all too often when dealing with the aristocracy, but it is only his way," Charles soothed.

"Yes, the perfect excuse for bad behaviour," Alfred responded. "Would you like me to accompany you on your search for a cottage?" he asked.

"No, thank you," Charles replied. "I had already heard of one, I was told about it while we were deciding on where Mr Lawson would live, so I will visit it before doing anything more. If it is not suitable, then I would welcome your help."

Alfred accepted what Charles had said and then left him, as it was time to visit Laura. Everyone knew what happened every afternoon, and accepted that it was a part of the complicated relationship that the two shared. Charles had some sympathy with the pair, but if anyone knew of his own inner turmoil they would surely wonder what on earth had happened at Home Farm since the visitors had arrived.

The following morning Charles set off the visit the cottage. It was only a few miles outside of the Home Farm Estate and so he took his time, enjoying the feeling of not being on the alert for Martha, every time he left a room, or rounded a corner.

The visit went well and he returned to the estate, taking the long way around. He almost groaned with frustration when he turned into one of the lanes and saw Martha walking ahead. He stopped his horse when he reached her and dismounted.

"Good morning Martha," he said.

"Good morning, Charles," Martha responded calmly enough, but her skin was flushed since the moment she had realised who was approaching her. "Did your journey prove fruitful?"

"Yes," Charles acknowledged. "The cottage is perfectly fine for mother and baby."

"Good, Laura will be relieved. I know she has suffered from feeling uncertain about her future, no matter how often I have tried to reassure her," Martha said

"I suppose it is easier to say words, than to believe them," came the obtuse response.

Martha flushed a little deeper, not sure whether it was a dig at her or not. "I'm sure," she murmured, but really did not wish to get into a deep conversation.

Charles changed the subject. "Have you responded to your brother yet?" What he really was asking was if she had sent the money to her family.

"Yes," came the quiet response.

Charles sighed, "Martha, I know he is your brother and you care for him, but he should not have asked you for such an amount."

Martha paused before replying. She actually agreed with Charles, Thomas could not help the situation they were in as such, but to ask a spinster for her life savings was condemning her to a life of goodness knew what struggles. As always though, Martha defended her brother. "We are a family and when one is trouble we help each other out."

Charles was stung a little at Martha's tone, "Well for your sake, and I mean this sincerely Martha, I hope he is there for you when it is your turn."

"Well I am sure that if he isn't, you will be standing in the background gloating," Martha snapped, always ready to imagine the worst in the man stood before her.

At her words, Charles stopped in his tracks and turned to face her. "I don't think I realised until today just how much you really do dislike me," he said, his face an astounded expression, as if he could not quite believe it.

"I don't," Martha said automatically, but there was no conviction in her words.

"Don't treat me as a fool Martha," Charles snapped. "Here I am, thinking that underneath the bluster, the criticism and the put downs, that you have some affection for me, but you don't, do you? You really must think me a cad if you would even consider that I would gloat at someone else's misfortunes."

"I don't think that!" Martha said quickly. "It is just that where I am concerned, I think you dislike me no matter what I say or do," she babbled.

"Where you are concerned?" Charles asked in disbelief. "I asked you to marry me, I kissed you, twice! How in the world would you think that I disliked you from those actions?"

"All your interference when we were last here and then at Dunham House, how could I not think that you disliked me?" Martha responded. "Whatever I did, you offered some comment or other, always interfering, always undermining."

"Interfering and undermining?" Charles spluttered. He looked at Martha, she looked mortified and uncomfortable. How had he managed to create this amount of animosity by his actions? He could not believe how wrong he had been. He sighed and shook his head. "I was foolish at the start of our acquaintance Martha and god help me, I have suffered for it since."

"I don't understand," Martha said, frowning and biting her lip.

"I saw you as this perfect woman, totally in control and a completely confident woman and clearly above my station. I wanted to ruffle your feathers. Maybe it was childish of me, but I did it out of attraction, I suppose. The problem I didn't foresee was your immediate dislike which developed because of my actions, and how that has remained firmly in place ever since. I have tried time and again to offer help and support and been rejected at every turn, but I still tried. I had no idea that your responses were genuine and that you can't abide me," Charles explained, finally being able to put into words what he had been feeling for months.

"I don't dislike you," Martha said quietly.

"Oh do me the honour of not treating me like an idiot as well," Charles said, his voice rising. "I tried to make amends for my foolishness and I thought, just the once at Dunham House, that I had succeeded, that you did think something of me, but I was obviously wrong. All that is now left for me to say is that I am sorry, for everything I have done, for making such a hash of things and choosing the one woman who was incapable of forgiveness. I sincerely apologise Martha, and please be assured that I will never trouble you again."

Charles mounted his horse and rode away, he had been a fool. The one woman he had to go and fall in love with and she would never, ever, consider him as a husband. What a damned mess.

Martha watched Charles ride away from her, rooted to the spot. He had said that he had been attracted to her from the start, she would never have imagined that his behaviour indicated that. Her head spun. He had liked her from the start?

Martha started to move towards the house. If Charles had liked her from the beginning, then that meant that his proposal was not so strange after all. She had condemned him for acting out of pity, when he must have been reacting on stronger feelings. Martha's cheeks stung with the deep red that infused them as she walked. Never in her life had she been so mortified at her behaviour. She had insulted the man who had been consistent in his regard.

She understood the kisses, they were no longer to be considered as something that had occurred because he was plaguing her, but because they meant something. She reflected on her own behaviour and it did not bode well. She had been rude, dismissive and angry and all without justification. If she had not been so precious about her ranking, her importance in the family, she probably would have seen Charles's actions for what they were.

She had responded to his kisses, and why? She had wanted them to happen, that was why, just as much as he had. Yes, they overwhelmed her, yes, the intensity frightened her, but she wanted them to happen. Just as in the same way that when she had seen him on his horse, her heart had started to pound, partly because she had expected him to stop and for a kiss to occur.

How arrogant she had been! How presumptuous, and how self-absorbed. The house came into sight, she could no longer hide the fact that most of the situation she was now in, losing the respect and affection of the one man who she cared for, was completely and utterly her own fault. She admitted to herself that she cared for him, how could she not? The acknowledgement could only add to her pain, it did not offer any comfort to her feelings.

After that first season, she had presumed that she would marry at some point, and look what had happened to bring her down to earth when she had been smug then. Her whole family had been almost ruined. She had accepted being a spinster, only allowing the longing for a husband and children to surface very occasionally and then be pushed down again, into the part of her heart that she rarely allowed out.

Then, after all this time, she had met a man, a handsome, charming man, who she was attracted to. If she could not openly acknowledge it, she could at least do so to herself after what had happened. She had been attracted to him from the start and his behaviour at the beginning had turned her against him. How foolish and childish had she acted, no better than a schoolroom miss.

Once again though, her smugness was being punished. Charles had withdrawn from her and would probably never speak to her again, never mind return to kiss her and ask her again to marry him. Her one chance of happiness and she had pushed at it until it was gone.

She returned to the house and sought the solace of her bed chamber, needing to gather herself a little before going to the drawing room. Martha looked at herself in the looking glass and groaned, she was not one for dramatic acts, but she was fairly sure that she would not be able to remain at Dunham House. She could not stay in the same employ as Charles, she would see him every day and it would be torture. If he found another woman to take as wife, she did not think she could bear to be reminded on a daily basis about what she had lost.

Yes, she would have to leave her beloved Elizabeth. Martha rested her head in her hands, she had destroyed everything in one sunny afternoon.

Chapter 18

Charles once again avoided Martha. He was beginning to act like a petulant child, but he honestly did not know what else to do. At least it was easier to avoid her with Lord and Lady Halkyn in the house. He could work alongside Lord Halkyn, or spend time at the cottage. He also started to arrange work on the cottage that Mr Lawson was to occupy, deciding that he needed to find a new steward, even if it meant that he employed someone for a short period. Little did they know it, but both parties were wishing for a return to Dunham House, but for different reasons.

Martha had decided that she needed to apologise to Charles, but there was no opportunity to do so. She could understand his reluctance to spend time with her, but it saddened her. She had completely lost him. Oh, he was polite enough when they were in the same company, but there was no longer that spark between them that Martha only realised had existed once it was gone.

She tried to busy herself, helping Laura whenever possible. Laura had ended her confinement and was looking forward to setting up home in the cottage. She had visited it on a number of occasions, a girl from the village was being employed to help with the baby, and then she would move with Laura to become a maid of all works. Laura had argued against such expense, but Lady Halkyn would hear none of it.

"Look on it as help for Frederica," Charlotte explained, as once again Laura had raised the issue of the maid. "She will want her Mama to help her, not to be spending all day cleaning the house."

"But I won't be working, Charlotte," Laura said. "I will have plenty of time."

"Grow flowers, sew, bake, or do anything that you enjoy," Charlotte said with a smile. "You are not going to win this argument, it is the least we can do."

"Thank you," Laura responded, reaching over and hugging her friend. "I don't care what the rules are on hugging a Lady, I will never stop! You really are being too kind."

"I can't take all the credit," Charlotte acknowledged with a smile. "Stephen is the one making most of the suggestions, I just agree with everything!"

"A happy marriage then," Laura teased.

"Oh, he doesn't get his own way all the time," Charlotte laughed. "He's far too stubborn for there not to be some conflict."

Laura smiled at her friend. "You are a very lucky girl, and I am happy for you Charlotte. I only knew Lord Halkyn a little before he met you, but you have brought out a nicer side to him."

"I hope so," Charlotte said, seriously. "I will never forget his laugh when I told him that you all said he was the kindest of the men that visited Baron Kersal's. He was so mocking about that. The reality was that you spoke the truth, he just didn't realise what you had all sensed." Charlotte was perfectly at ease with the fact that Lord Halkyn had visited brothels before their marriage. Lord Halkyn doted on his wife and made it clear to all and sundry, which was even more of a surprise, as he had previously been the biggest critic of anyone who had openly shown affection for their spouse.

*

Laura climbed into the cart that Martha was about to drive to the cottage. "I think there mustn't be anything left in Home Farm with the things that are packed in here," Laura said with a shake of her head in wonder. Furniture and supplies had been bought and Lady Dunham, although many hundreds of miles away, had sent instructions about what items were to be sent to the cottage.

"I think there will be just enough room for you and Frederica to squeeze in, once everything is in place," Martha smiled.

"I hope so," Laura said excitedly. "I know my removal will mean you all will be deserting me, but I am looking forward to settling in." She had almost accepted that Alfred would be leaving in the next few days. There was a tiny part of her that hoped he would stay with her, but her sensible side knew that he would return to London and continue his employment with Bow Street.

He would always be the love of her life, but she was pragmatic about the fact that they were not destined to be together. At least she would have Frederica, something that she would never regret, especially as every time she looked into her baby's eyes, Alfred's looked back at her. She would treasure her daughter and in her own way, treasure the man who had created her.

They had not yet had an opportunity to speak about the connection between Alfred and Frederica. Laura was choosing her time carefully, but she had the feeling that Alfred would never quite believe her, if she told him again that he was Frederica's father, which saddened her and delayed her raising the subject. At the moment, it was just a fear that Alfred would not believe her, but once the words were said, there would be no going back.

They reached the cottage in good time and found Charles, speaking with a gardener, who was to clear the cottage garden and then the responsibility lay with Laura as to what it needed and for its general upkeep. Charles nodded his welcome, but did not stop in his task. Martha flushed a little, but put her head down and carried on with her own business. During the past few days she had not been able to look at Charles because of the shame she felt.

Charles popped his head in the cottage doorway and looked at Laura, "Is there anything you would like assistance with before I head back to Home Farm?" he asked pleasantly, but he did not look in Martha's direction.

"No, thank you Charles, I think we have everything under control," Laura responded with a smile. She was thoroughly enjoying seeing the house emerge into a home.

"Very well, I shall see you both on your return," Charles said with a slight bow and left the ladies.

"He's a nice man," Laura said, as she continued to unpack.

Martha did not respond. She had been blind to how nice Charles actually was and would feel like a hypocrite if she started to sing his praises now.

The two women worked together all afternoon, until the house looked like it was ready to welcome its new occupants. Laura stood back surveying the room. The range filled one side of the wall, a dresser filling the shorter wall, now adorned with plates. The sink was situated under the window, overlooking the garden. A table filled the centre of the room, along with two comfortable chairs that were near the range, perfect for cosy evenings in front of the warmth.

Laura closed the door and locked it, putting the key in the apron that was protecting her dress. "I think it is ready to move into. The beds are arriving tomorrow and then it just our clothes and that is everything. I've never owned so many things in my life," she said, feeling content and happy.

"It is a lovely cottage," Martha said. "You need to bring some of the flowers from the estate to put in the garden and then it will be complete."

"I will," Laura said, climbing into the cart.

Martha took the reins and started back to the estate. The women talked about what Laura could do with the garden, as the horse made steady progress through the lanes.

Turning from the main route, onto the outside edge of the estate, the horse was frightened and Martha struggled to keep control. When it eventually came to a reluctant stop she climbed down to soothe the animal.

"What's wrong with him?" Laura asked.

"No idea, but something spooked him, he's fine now though, aren't you boy?" Martha said stroking the horse's nose.

Martha heard a sound behind her, but before she could turn, she was grabbed around the neck and pulled backwards away from the horse. She went very still as she felt something cold against her neck and had the stinging sensation of being cut.

"Afternoon ladies," came a distinctly London voice.

Both women did not respond, each looking at the other in horror. "So sorry to have to interrupt your excursion, but I have unfinished business with one of you."

Laura slowly stepped out of the cart, knowing immediately that she had been found. "Leave her alone," she said. "It's me you want, not her."

"No!" Martha hissed at her friend. Martha had realised, like Laura, that someone or something had led him to Laura, but as long as he did not know which of them Laura was, there was a chance that she would be safe.

"Do I now?" the man asked. "That's very obliging of you."

Martha tried to twist her head a little towards him. "Spare us and you will be well rewarded by Lord Halkyn," she said, trying to use the only thing she could think of that would save them. She prayed that someone would think of something that needed to be taken to the cottage and their paths would cross.

"Will I?" he asked, looking interestedly at Martha. "How much?"

"As much as it takes," Martha said, trying to memorise every detail of his face, although it was partially covered to prevent identification. Martha knew that she had to try and recall it, if they did get out alive.

"And as soon as I approach the house, they would have me in chains and I would be swinging quicker than you could say how much. Do you take me for a fool?" he spat, holding the knife harder against Martha's neck.

Martha could not swallow if she had wished, for fear that the knife would severe something vital and she would bleed to death on the roadside. "No!" she croaked, desperate to calm him down.

"Stop!" Laura shouted out, moving closer. "Your argument is with me, let her be."

"Brave little thing aren't you? No wonder you got away from me last time," he said with an almost admiring tone.

"Are you the man that I saw on the wharf?" Laura asked, suddenly feeling resigned.

"I am," came the clipped response.

"I didn't recognise you, you were in the shadows then," Laura said calmly, almost as if she was having an everyday conversation with a passer-by.

"You should have let me catch you then, it would have been over and done with in a second," the man responded, as conversationally as Laura.

"I could not let you kill my child," Laura said simply.

The man moved Martha over towards Laura, Martha mouthed 'run' to her friend, but Laura shook her head slightly. There was no running, there was no escape. She had been foolish to think that she could escape, when in reality the networks that existed could never been overcome by a lowly woman like herself.

She had achieved what she had set out to do, Frederica was safe and would be well cared for, she had done her duty. Yes, she wanted to live, wanted to with every fibre of her being, but she was not about to sacrifice Martha for an attempt at an escape. It was not as if she had anywhere to go to. She had no other connections than the ones who had offered support now, if they could not protect her, no one could.

When her assailant was within a few inches, he stopped. "No one usually gets away from me, you should be proud of yourself," he said and then acted quickly. He threw Martha to one side, unbalancing her and sending her sprawling across the ground. At the same moment, he lunged at Laura and buried the knife deep into her stomach. It was a well aimed lunge, as the knife was inserted below Laura's stays, which could have protected her if the knife had been inserted slightly higher.

He withdrew the knife and watched while Laura sank to her knees, all colour fading from her face. Only when she slumped to the floor did he take off at a run through the hedgerow.

Chapter 19

Martha crawled across to Laura's slumped shape. She could feel the trickle of blood down her neck, but she disregarded it. "Laura?" she croaked.

Laura was still, but Martha could see that she was still breathing. She had to get her back into the cart. She turned her body over and gasped when she saw the wound. It was on the right of Laura's body and was oozing a lot of blood. Laura had groaned when she had been moved, so at least Martha knew she was conscious.

Martha ran to the cart and grabbed their shawls, she folded one and placed it over the wound. She reached for Laura's hand and placed it over the temporary bandage.

"Laura, can you hear me? I need you to press against this, with all your might. Do you understand?"

Laura pressed obediently, but did not respond. Martha gritted her teeth. She was determined to get Laura back to the house, where help was, but she was not sure if she was able to get her into the cart.

"I need to move you Laura," she said, her voice gentle. "Laura, this is going to hurt, but I need you to work with me."

Martha struggled with the young woman, more than once nearly sagging to the ground in defeat. All the time, she muttered words of comfort, to try and reassure Laura that they were achieving their aim.

After what seemed like hours, Martha slumped against the end of the cart. She had managed to bundle Laura into the back and had used the empty sacks to try and cushion her. She covered her with the spare shawl and ran to the front of the cart, quickly picking up the reins and starting the journey back to the estate.

Martha travelled as fast as she dared, all the time, shouting words of comfort or instruction over her shoulder. Very often she had to act like an angry school teacher, shouting commands, when it looked like the pressure of Laura's hand was easing from the shawl pressing on the wound.

The journey seemed to take an eternity, but eventually Martha turned onto the lane that led to the side of the house. She started to shout for help, while at the same time as sending reassuring comments to Laura.

The noise that Martha made, caused staff and guests to come running to the front of the house. Lord Halkyn and Alfred were the first to react to Martha's words. She was shouting that Laura was injured, that she needed help. The pair ran to the back of the cart, their faces setting grimly at the scene that greeted them, and carried Laura inside.

Charles had stood transfixed at the sight before him. Martha had a cut of six inches across her throat, from which blood was dripping down onto the front of her dress. That would have been horrifying enough for the man, standing there watching the scene, but her skirts were covered in blood as well. He felt the bile rise in his throat as the reality of Martha being injured hit him.

"Charles! Here, now!" Lord Halkyn shouted. They were trying to carry Laura in without causing her any more pain than they had to and they needed a third a person to help.

Lord Halkyn's voice roused Charles and he ran across to the cart. The three men carried Laura into her bedchamber and laid her carefully in the bed. A doctor had already been sent for by Smithson, ever responsive to any situation.

"What happened?" Lord Halkyn asked Martha.

"The man who was following her in London, he found us," she replied, not able to take her eyes off Laura, her skin was ghostly white.

"Can you describe him?" Alfred asked, trying to remain focused, but deep down knowing what Laura's injury meant.

"He was covered," Martha frowned trying to remember, "But when I turned my head slightly, I saw he had a scar from his ear to his chin."

"Are you sure?" Alfred snapped, for the first time looking away from Laura.

"Yes, it was most peculiar, but I only saw it that once, as I said, he was covered up," Martha responded. "Laura said she had not recognised him immediately because the last time she had seen him, he had been standing in the shadows."

"Damn it!" Alfred muttered to himself, but Lord Halkyn raised his eyebrows at him.

"We shall discuss this when the Doctor arrives," Lord Halkyn said to Alfred.

The doctor arrived in record time and all left the room, apart from Martha and Charlotte. The gentlemen retired to the study, where Lord Halkyn poured three large brandies.

"You recognised the attacker from the description that Miss Fairfield gave you," Lord Halkyn said to Alfred. It was not a question, but a statement.

"Yes," Alfred said, drinking the brandy in one gulp.

"Is he a well known criminal?" Lord Halkyn asked.

"He's a Bow Street Officer," Alfred said quietly.

"What?" Charles exclaimed.

"Yes, one of the people who is meant to protect others, and instead he was apparently going around doing the killing. If he admitted he was the one Laura saw following her, he has killed at least one other and probably two other women," Alfred said, looking into his empty glass without really seeing. "And I brought him here."

"How did you do that?" Charles asked, not believing Alfred's words, he had never known such an upstanding man.

"I wrote to my senior, Mr Frost didn't I? Asking when I was expected to return to work. It wouldn't be very hard for someone working on the inside to access Mr Frost's office and access the information. No one would have suspected Corless."

"Corless? Do I know that name?" Lord Halkyn asked with a frown.

"Yes," Alfred said bitterly. "He was the one working on the outside, when I was on the inside at Baron Kersal's. Perfect really, he will have known exactly who was who, so when the time came to get rid of them, his job would have been even easier."

"Do you think Kersal knew beforehand what we were doing?" Lord Halkyn asked.

"Probably not," Alfred admitted. "But if you remember, I was kept well out of the way when the raid took place, and Corless led it. He would have had a lot of contact with the Baron, ample time for him to be persuaded to help the criminal, apparently."

"What a bloody disaster," Lord Halkyn said with a whoosh of breath.

"That, my Lord, is the understatement of the year," Alfred responded bitterly, before putting his head in his hands.

When the doctor returned downstairs, Alfred went out to meet him. Lord Halkyn let him go, he had a good idea of what Alfred and Laura felt about each other and was willing for Alfred to take charge of the care needed for Laura. He came back into the library and went to the brandy decanter, poured himself a large glass and for the second time that day, drank it in one gulp.

Lord Halkyn and Charles looked at each other, but Lord Halkyn broke the silence. "Alfred?" he asked.

Alfred did not turn to face them, maintaining his stance near the drinks cabinet. "There is no hope, it is just a matter of time," he said quietly.

"I'm sorry," Lord Halkyn said. "You had better go to her."

"Yes," Alfred agreed and left the room, leaving the two men to dwell on their own thoughts.

The bedchamber was still when Alfred entered, he did not knock and wait to be admitted, there was no longer time for formalities. He had known what the outcome would be as soon as he had seen Laura, he had seen knife wounds before. Once in a major organ, there was very little hope and Laura's wound was so deep and wide, it could not have missed something vital. Fool that he was, a tiny part of him had hoped, no, had prayed, that for once he would be proved wrong. That the doctor would come to him and say that in time she would recover.

He walked over to the bed and Martha moved to let him have access, it was obvious she had been crying, Alfred did not know how he was managing not to, but he just stood still, looking down at the love of his life. Charlotte was holding one of Laura's hands, quietly crying.

Laura's red hair was scattered across the pillow, as if she had just fallen backwards in laughter, but there were no smiles around her lips today. Her colouring was grey, that of death, rather than life. Her eyes normally so vibrant and expressive were closed, in pain, if the frown across her forehead was anything to go by. She still wore the dress she had been brought in with, there was hardly any indication of what colour it had been, there was so much blood and dirt intermingled in the material.

Alfred reached down and touched Laura's hand gently. "Now then woman, what's all this fuss you are creating?" he said, but his voice was husky with restrained tears.

Laura did not quite open her eyes, but they fluttered and her lips twitched. Alfred felt as if his heart was physically being ripped out, his chest hurt so much.

"If you'd have asked for me to stay a few extra days, I would have you know," he gently chided. "There was no need to make all this fuss."

Laura's lips twitched again, but this time she squeezed at his hand, as if she wanted him to come closer. Alfred put his face close to hers. Laura frowned deeper and gritted her teeth. "Frederica," she whispered. The word cost her a great deal, because she gasped in agony when she had uttered it.

Alfred, remained close to Laura's face and said quietly. "She is safe Laura, and always will be. I promise you, she will be well looked after and cared for. She will be loved like she deserves, *I* will care for her. Do you understand what I am saying Laura, do you understand?" he asked, his voice urgent, but clear.

Laura nodded her head slightly and once again the smile touched her lips.

The group stayed by the bedside, maintaining the bandage on the wound, but not able to do anything else to help their friend. As the minutes passed it was obvious she was getting weaker, as her breath was becoming more shallow and laboured.

Alfred was surprised that she had survived so long, it just showed what a strong, determined woman she was. He tried to imprint her image into his mind, but in reality he knew that he would never forget, could never forget any detail of her.

She muttered something and he leaned closer to her. "What is it, Laura?" he asked.

Laura seemed to need a certain amount of air before she could speak and took some gasps that were deeper than the ones she had been previously taking. She turned to Alfred and opened her eyes slowly, looking at him through the curtain of pain that was enveloping her.

She took another breath and with a wistful smile said, "In another life....." before the effort became too much.

Alfred's eyes filled with tears that this time spilled onto his cheeks, but he smiled at the woman on the bed. "In another life....." he said and kissed her cheek.

Laura closed her eyes with a sigh and her breathing stopped.

Chapter 20

Charles knocked on the door of Martha's bedchamber and entered when he heard her voice. Everyone had retired, to be alone with their thoughts and grief, but Charles had been unable to settle knowing that Martha was upset and injured.

Martha sat in front of her looking glass, trying to brush her hair out, but in reality, sitting and crying. She did not react when Charles entered the room, or when he closed the door behind him and turned the key in the lock. She just looked at him with eyes full of tears.

"Oh Martha, my love," Charles said, crossing the room in three strides, "Come here." He lifted her from the chair and wrapped her in his arms.

His words and actions were the catalyst that tipped Martha over the edge and she sobbed into his shoulder, while he stroked her back, not making any sounds, letting her grieve in her own way. They stood like that for some time, before Martha gathered herself enough to lean away slightly from Charles and dry her eyes.

"I'm sorry," she whispered.

"Don't ever be sorry for caring for someone," Charles responded, slowly brushing Martha's hair away from her shoulder. He had never seen it down, it fell below her shoulders, softening her face, making her seem younger and more vulnerable.

"I couldn't get her back any quicker," she said, hanging her head. "I didn't want to hurt her even more."

"You could have done no more," Charles said, reassuringly, lifting her chin, forcing her to meet his gaze. "The wound was delivered to kill, Martha, and there was nothing any of us could have done to help her."

"I didn't want her to tell him which one he was looking for, I thought it may have given her more time to escape," Martha said, explaining some of the angst that she was feeling.

Charles went cold at her words. She had been willing to put herself at risk to try and help Laura. "He had seen her before," Charles said. "But you did get injured," he said noticing again the cut on her neck. It had not been cleaned up, Martha had been unable to let anyone touch her while her friend lay dying.

"Sit." Charles commanded, gently forcing Martha to sit on the dressing table stool. He walked over to the wash basin and poured some fresh water from the nearby jug, before carrying the basin over and placing it on the dressing table. Taking his handkerchief out of his pocket, he dipped it into the water.

"Raise your head, I want to clean the wound," he instructed, his voice firm, but kind.

"I can do it," Martha said, but lifted her head anyway.

"For once, let me look after you without an argument," Charles responded, but he smiled and placed a chaste kiss on her forehead.

Martha closed her eyes and allowed Charles to minister to her. She felt so drained, while so many possibilities and questions went around and around in her mind until she felt that it might explode. The gentle movement made by Charles, soothed her thoughts, as well as cleaned her body.

When he had finished, the bowl was deep red and her dress front was wet. "I'm sorry about your dress, you need to change into your night things," Charles said.

"What?" Martha gasped, her eyes snapping open.

"Don't worry," Charles smiled in amusement. "You are safe, even I am not so base as to be anything other than a gentleman today. Go behind the screen and get changed."

Martha obeyed him, feeling shame that once again she had presumed his words had meant something which they did not. When she had secured her robe around her, she peeped around the edge of the room divider.

"What now?" she asked, her cheeks flushed.

"You come and sit at your dressing table and I will brush your hair," Charles instructed, indicating with his hand, where he wanted her.

"Charles, you really don't have to...." Martha started, but was quickly interrupted.

"If you say I don't have to once more, I will lay you over my knees and give you the tanning you are so obviously short of," he said, still trying to be gentle, but frustration getting the better of him.

Martha flushed deeper, but moved across to the dressing table chair. "I don't want you to feel obliged, that's all," she said a little defensively.

"I don't feel obliged," Charles said firmly. "I am here because I want to be, I don't need to repeat myself do I?"

"No," Martha said meekly, closing her eyes and allowing herself to relax.

Charles took hold of Martha's hair and forced himself not to bring it up to his face to feel the texture. He would be the type of person that Martha thought he was if he did anything inappropriate today, so he restrained himself and concentrated on slow, long brush strokes. He felt her tension easing away, as little by little the hair became a smooth curtain.

Eventually he placed the brush down on the dressing table and put his hands on Martha's shoulders, looking at her through the looking glass. "You need to rest now," he said gently.

"I feel exhausted, but I don't want to sleep," Martha admitted.

"You have had a shock, you need to rest. Come, to bed with you, young lady," Charles instructed.

Martha smiled a little at the term he used and allowed herself to be led by the hand to her bed. The whole situation was very strange, but somehow after the events of the day, it was comforting to be taken care of and not have to think. She climbed into bed and Charles pulled the covers over her.

Charles bent over and kissed Martha on the lips, it was a gentle, loving kiss that would not lead to anything more. "Get some rest. If you need me, just send for me, at any time," he said.

"Thank you," Martha said quietly, flushing a little at his closeness and the feelings he stirred. She did not want to start a big conversation, but she could not help uttering, "I'm sorry," to him as he straightened.

"What for?" Charles asked with a frown.

"For everything," Martha responded quietly.

"You are safe, and right now I need nothing more," Charles said with feeling. "Goodnight Martha."

Martha watched his retreating figure, before closing her eyes. The day had been horrific and she would mourn Laura's passing, but she felt secure and safe and that was due to Charles Anderton. She closed her eyes and drifted to sleep.

*

Charles found Lord Halkyn sitting in the study. Charlotte had remained in their bedchamber having cried herself to sleep, her guilt over the whole episode being more than she could bear. Charles poured himself a drink, before joining the Lord in front of the fire.

"Where is Alfred?" Charles asked, worried about the young man.

"I'm here," came a voice from the doorway. Alfred looked pale and drawn, but entered the room and sat near the gentlemen.

158

"Glad you are," Lord Halkyn responded. "We need to discuss what happens about Corless."

"There is no point sending a letter," Alfred said bitterly, "we know that method is not secure. He must feel that he cannot be identified, or I am sure he would not have left Martha alive."

Charles took a sharp intake of breath, he had thought the same, but having it voiced made it feel more like a real danger.

Both men heard the reaction, but ignored it, there were too many emotions alive that evening for anyone to comment, or tease someone about the way they were feeling.

"If he thinks he is safe that will make him careless, which can only be to our advantage. We have no guarantee that he will return to the Bow Street Offices, if he returns to London at all," Lord Halkyn mused.

"It is a perfect situation to be in," Alfred countered. "If he is in the pay of the likes of Baron Kersal, being at Bow Street will give him access to information that can only help the Baron and his cronies." It was a perfect set up, someone on the inside, someone who no one had ever suspected. Alfred cursed the day he had sent that letter, especially as in reality he had never wanted to leave anyway.

"Well in that case when you return to London, I shall leave it for you to deal with as you see fit," Lord Halkyn said, knowing how capable the officer was.

"I won't be returning to London," Alfred responded.

"What?" Lord Halkyn said in surprise. Charles did not look surprised, just thoughtful.

"I promised Laura that I would look after her child and that is what I am going to do," Alfred explained, the expression in his eyes, almost challenging the peer of the realm sat before him.

"The child would be safe here, while you returned. When Corless is sorted out, you can return to the child then," Lord Halkyn said, dismissively.

"I promised that the child will be safe and by my returning to London, she may not be. We know how determined Corless is, I am no coward, but I have lost too many people to the likes of him. From now on, I am going to look after myself and the baby, away from that hell-hole that is London," Alfred said firmly. He had made some mistakes in his life, some of which he would pay for the rest of his days, but he was determined to do the right thing by Frederica.

"Well," Lord Halkyn said, a little at a loss. "That changes everything. I suppose you expect me to fix things as usual?"

A small smile appeared on Alfred's lips, knowing full well the words were said in jest. "Yes, I suppose I do, my Lord," he said.

"If I could interrupt," Charles said, "It would be no trouble for me to go to London, before returning to Dunham House. Lord and Lady Dunham are still in the city, so it would make sense for me to travel there anyway. I can visit the Bow Street Offices while in London, with the support of Lord Dunham."

"Good, that's settled then," Lord Halkyn said. "Everything sorted without any effort on my part, just as I like it." His words hid the sadness that the day's events had caused. He owed a lot to Laura, as he had acknowledged in the past. By saving his Charlotte from a forced marriage, she had ultimately lost her life and her child was now motherless. It would be a long time before he could think about that without being angry and upset, feelings he was not used to having about people unrelated to him. His words were said for effect and were appreciated by the two men. The mind screams for normality when the situation is too horrific to bear.

Chapter 21

The following few days passed in a haze for the occupants of Home Farm. Laura was buried at the local church, not too far away from the cottage that she had so looked forward to living in. Lord and Lady Halkyn arranged to leave, once Charlotte was sure that Frederica would be cared for.

Lord Halkyn approached Alfred the day before their departure. "I need to arrange for the money I was to give to Laura, to be passed onto yourself," he said, watching with amusement at Alfred's stiffening posture at his words.

"I don't need your money, I can provide for the child," Alfred snapped in response.

"Maybe, maybe not, I'm not really interested, but my wife wants to know that the child is well provided for," Lord Halkyn responded.

"She will be," Alfred almost snarled. "I promised Laura and I will do right by her memory and the baby."

Lord Halkyn sighed. Being decent really was still a struggle for him, but he had to respond to the young man before him with some sensitivity. "Alfred, this is not a slur on your ability to provide for the child, we just want to help."

"There is no need," Alfred responded belligerently.

"There is every need," Lord Halkyn said. "Do you realise what a debt I owe to Laura?" he asked. "Ultimately, it has cost her life, but yet I have gained a wife, who people keep telling me has been the making of me."

"She has been," Alfred responded gruffly.

Lord Halkyn's eyebrow twitched with amusement. "If not for your commitment to the child, we would take her in as one of our own, that is how seriously I am treating this."

Alfred looked surprised and shocked at the statement and looked about to speak, but before he could, Lord Halkyn continued.

"The least we can do is ensure she has the best schooling and a dowry that will secure her future, and although you are being honourable and decent, don't spoil the effect by also being a fool," Lord Halkyn finished.

"And I thought you were being nice," Alfred said, amused.

"I find if I am consistently nice, it makes me feel nauseous," came the quick reply. "So, can I reassure my wife that you will accept the funds to ensure that the child secures a good marriage when she is of age?"

"Yes," Alfred replied. He would care for Frederica as he had promised, but part of that care was to provide a decent future for her and he could not provide the dowry that Lord and Lady Halkyn would be able to.

"Good," Lord Halkyn replied.

Any further conversation was prevented by the entrance of Smithson, who informed the gentlemen that a Mr Frost had called and asked to speak to Alfred.

"Well, well, it looks like Corless may not be as good as he thought he was," Lord Halkyn said. "Show the man in Smithson," he commanded.

Alfred refrained from reminding the Lord that Corless had probably killed at least four women, it was pointless trying to make someone so far removed from his own background understand the real impact that Corless's actions had. Ultimately he decided it was easier to save his breath.

Mr Frost was led into the drawing room, along with another officer, a Mr Henshaw. Introductions were made, before Mr Frost explained the reason for the visit.

"We have a traitor in our midst," Mr Frost said.

"Corless," Alfred said dully.

Mr Frost looked at the young man and noticed the haunted look in his expression, the black rings underneath his eyes and in his usual quick way, made a fair assessment of the situation. "We are too late?" he asked Alfred.

"Yes," Alfred said. "He visited us a few days ago."

"Damn it! I'm sorry Alfred, we thought we would catch him before he reached here," Mr Frost said, frustration and anger showing on his face. "The woman?"

"Laura is dead," Alfred said dully.

"Corless?" Mr Frost snapped, not angry with Alfred, but with himself at the decisions he had made.

"He's gone, escaped on the day he killed her," Lord Halkyn said. "We were working on the principle that he and you had no idea we knew who he was, so we could catch up with him at any point."

"I'm hoping that is still the case my Lord," Mr Frost responded. "I had suspected that something wasn't right, information seemed to be falling into the wrong hands. When you left, Alfred, I looked into things and events didn't add up quite as they should have done. It wasn't very long before I had to acknowledge that someone within the team was connected, although initially I had no idea who that person could be. Once I realised there was a leak though, it wasn't hard to work out who," he said.

"As I was here protecting Laura, for all the good I did, I'm sure it wasn't," Alfred responded.

"Yes, if the rotten egg was you, we would never have heard about Laura in the first place," Mr Frost acknowledged. "There was only Corless who had any real dealings with the case, apart from yourself. I had to make sure it was him though, as I couldn't accuse him of falsehood without being sure of my facts first. Unfortunately, by the time I was sure, I had received your letter."

"And he had seen it, which led him straight to us," Alfred finished.

"I guessed as much and set out immediately, but it looks as if he saw it a lot sooner than I anticipated. I am truly sorry that we didn't arrive in time," Mr Frost said again.

"He was determined to finish the job," Alfred acknowledged.

"But we can finish him," Mr Frost said, already standing to leave. "We shan't delay any longer. If we return immediately, we have a chance of finding him before he realises we are on to him. I shall await your return to London when you are ready."

"I was going to write to you," Alfred said. "I won't be returning to my employment, or to the city."

Mr Frost held out his hand. "I had wished for better for you Alfred. You are a fine officer, but I didn't want you to return, that life is no good for a fine young man such as yourself. I had hoped that you would find a better life here. I am sorry it has not worked out that way."

Alfred flushed a little, it was obvious that his employer had some suspicions about his relationship with Laura. "I am sorry too," he responded gruffly, shaking the hand offered.

"I wish you all the very best," Mr Frost said. "I shall let you know when we have charged Corless, don't doubt that he will receive justice for what he has done. Gentlemen," he finished with a bow and left the room.

*

Alfred had kept away from Frederica's room. He could not bear to look at the child in the first few days after Laura had died, in case she reminded him of her mother. He did not think that his mind could cope with seeing Laura's likeness without being able to reach her.

A wet nurse had been employed to feed the child, once her mother was no longer alive and between the maid, the wet nurse, Martha and Charlotte, the baby suffered no neglect.

164

The evening after Lord and Lady Halkyn had left Home Farm, Alfred restlessly walked the hallways of the house. He could not settle and did not know why. Time and again, he found himself outside the nursery, but unable to open the door and walk in.

As he stood once more on the threshold, he was startled when the young maid opened the door on him. She was as equally surprised. "Oh sir, I'm sorry, I wasn't expecting you," she apologised moving out of Alfred's way. "I'm just going to the kitchen, do you need me sir?"

"No," Alfred responded. "I was about to visit the child," he said, a little unsure of what to say.

"Oh good, I hope you don't mind, but I have a few things I'd like to do, but I don't like leaving her for too long. Would you be happy to stay until I returned? The wet nurse has left a list of things for me to arrange before she returns," the young maid explained.

Alfred felt a little panicked about being asked to stay on his own in the room with a baby and some of his fear must have shown on his face as the maid smiled in reassurance. "Oh don't worry sir, she's a good little thing, doesn't wake until she needs feeding, not a spot of bother at all."

"Fine," Alfred said gruffly and moved into the room.

The maid left the door a little ajar and Alfred was alone. He approached the cradle slowly, not wanting to be the cause of waking the baby after such praise from the maid.

The child was fast asleep, one hand scrunched into a fist near her face, as if she was in the process of shaking it at someone. Alfred smiled a little, just like her fiery mother then.

Her hair was dark, not red as he had expected, so he was not struck by Laura's likeness. It still did not ease the tightness in his chest that increased as he continued to stand over her, his mind racing at the 'what ifs' that would now never be answered.

A sound at the door, disturbed him and he looked up, expecting to see the maid returning, but was surprised to see Martha coming quietly into the room. She smiled slightly at him and moved to the opposite side of the cradle.

"She's beautiful, isn't she?" Martha asked, knowing that this was the first time that Alfred had seen the child since Laura's death.

"Yes," he responded quietly.

"Alfred, I am so sorry that I couldn't do more to save Laura," Martha said, quiet enough not to wake the child, but Alfred heard the sob in her voice.

He looked at the woman who had become a friend over the weeks that they had lived together. "We are all sorry that we could not do more Martha," he responded.

"She was so happy about having her own home," Martha said, wiping her eyes.

"Yes, I know," Alfred said. A home that he knew she wanted to share with him, he thought bitterly at his stupidity.

"She would have spoiled Frederica," Martha smiled at the child. "She told me that having her was everything she had ever wanted."

"I suppose it came of having no family of her own," Alfred responded.

"That and who the father was," Martha said tentatively. It was not her place to interfere, but she thought that she owed it to Laura to make sure that Alfred was under no doubt about his relationship with the baby. It was too important after everything that had happened.

Alfred glanced sharply at Martha. He wanted to walk out of the room, his heart was pounding so much, but he stayed rooted to the spot. "How do you know that she told you the truth?" he asked.

"Laura didn't lie," Martha said, in her quiet, but firm way. "She had no reason to. Frederica was the only child she ever had, you know."

166

Alfred nodded his head. Laura had never said as much, but he knew from her behaviour that she had never had another child. If she had, he was sure that she would have found a way to keep it.

Martha flushed a little at what she was going to say, she was not used to being so bold, let alone so bold in front of a gentleman. "She once told me that there were ways that the women in her profession could prevent babies. I don't know the details, but it must be true, or they would be constantly with child."

"I suppose so," Alfred responded, but he had winced at the thought of Laura with other men.

"The Baron had moved her into looking after the younger girls long before she made the decision to have the baby," Martha continued, telling Alfred something that he already knew. "But when she had the opportunity of the one chance of being with the man she cared about, she took the opportunity that would give her the thing she wanted from the man she loved."

"Martha, stop," Alfred said, his voice cracking.

"You do know that Frederica is your child, don't you?" Martha persisted.

"She shouted it at me once," Alfred admitted, "but I didn't believe her. Well that's not exactly true," Alfred acknowledged. "After she gave birth, she said that we would talk about it, but it is too late now," he said.

"She told me," Martha admitted. "Well, I guessed and she confirmed it. She said that she'd told you and you didn't believe her, but please believe what she told you," she insisted.

"What difference does it make now?" Alfred responded dejectedly.

"It makes a huge difference to Frederica," Martha said. "Alfred, she is your child, there is no doubt that Laura was telling the truth. You need to accept that you are the father of this little girl and tell the world that she is yours. She needs to feel secure as she grows, believe me. I have seen the damage that can be done when a child feels as if the parent is disappointed in her," Martha said, referring to the hurt that she had seen in her employer, Lady Dunham, due to the fact that her father had wanted a boy.

"She is more likely to be disappointed in me," Alfred said. "I have no idea what to do with a child, Martha."

Martha sensed the panic in his voice and reached over to squeeze his arm. "No parent knows what to do when it is their first child. You will have the support around you which you require, all you need to do is to love her and accept her, and the rest you will work out together."

Martha reached over and scooped up the baby into her arms and walked around the cradle. Alfred looked alarmed, but did not pull away when she handed him the child. "Frederica, it's time to meet your Papa," Martha said softly, letting go of the baby when she was sure Alfred held her securely.

Alfred stood stiffly, almost afraid to breathe, as the child snuggled to get comfortable once more. He seemed to relax slightly when he rocked her gently and she settled into sleep once more.

"See, you are an expert already," Martha reassured him. "I shall leave you two together, you have a lot of catching up to do."

Alfred was left alone in the room once more, staring down at the bundle in his arms. He continued to rock her gently, afraid that if he stopped, she would wake once more. As he gained a little more confidence, his hand stroked the side of her face, feeling the softness and marvelling at her tiny hand.

"Hello Frederica, my little girl," he said quietly, as the tears rolled unchecked down his face.

Chapter 22

Charles handed Martha the letter. He recognised the handwriting of her brother and wanted to force her to open it in front of him, but she had learned from the last time, and saved the letter until she was alone. With everything that had been happening, Martha had not written as much as she normally did, since she did not want to burden Thomas with a letter that would make him worry about her, he already had enough to deal with. So she waited until she was seated on her window seat in her bed chamber and read the letter.

Later Martha would reflect that it was a wise decision to read the letter away from Charles Anderton, for it would surely have convinced him that she was a selfish woman who he should avoid. Thomas had written that Susan was to be married. She had met a gentleman related to the family whom she was employed by, and he had asked her to marry him. Thomas wrote that the couple seemed very well suited and were very much in love, and that they wanted Martha to attend the wedding if possible.

Martha was delighted for her sister, she truly was, but she could not prevent the pang of envy that shot through her the first time she read the letter. Susan was to be married, she would leave the life of an employee behind her and no doubt soon have a family of her own, to have everything that Martha had hoped for. Martha was envious of the situation, not of her sister, who she loved dearly.

She looked out of the window and smiled slightly to herself. If she had truly wanted a marriage, she had received the proposal from Charles, she should have accepted it and be done. Charles, bless him! She had accused him of offering for her out of pity, and although she had ranted at him for doing so, it was a gallant gesture. She sighed, she had been foolish with Charles, her first impressions had been wrong and she had acted in a way that had probably cost her the only chance of happiness that she would ever have.

Martha stood and smoothed down her dress, there was no point in crying over what could have been. She had acted in a way which would keep her on the path she had chosen. That would not prevent her from trying to join her family, or enjoying her sister's happiness. She left her room to seek out Charles.

He was working in the study as usual when Martha entered. She explained what the letter contained.

"I need to write to Lady Dunham, to ask if she can spare me for a little while longer. I don't suppose there would be much of a problem, they seem settled in London," Martha said.

"Yes, for the first time, they seem to be enjoying their visit," Charles agreed, surprised that his employers had remained in London for so long when they usually avoided the place. "When is the wedding?"

"They are getting a special licence, so it is in less than a week," Martha explained. "At least the journey from here to Cheshire won't be too tedious."

"Why don't I accompany you?" Charles offered. He did not want Martha to travel alone, but it was for selfish reasons that he spoke up.

"What about finding a steward?" Martha asked understandably, as nothing had been achieved in replacing Mr Lawson.

"I have a solution to that," Charles explained. "All I need to do is to speak to Alfred."

"Alfred?" Martha asked, before realising the plan behind the words. "Oh, what an excellent idea!" she said with a beaming smile.

Charles's chest squeezed with pleasure at being the cause of such a positive response from Martha, and smiled in return. "If Alfred agrees, we could set off in the morning, since there would be nothing further holding us here."

Martha was a little torn, her family would wonder at her travelling with Charles, although if their visit was on the way back to Dunham House, it would not be considered all that unusual. She would like his company, if she was honest with herself, because his teasing manner would stop her from falling into the doldrums. Those were the reasons she told herself anyway. If there was any other motivation behind her feelings, she was not ready to acknowledge them.

"If Alfred agreed, we could stay for a few days with my family, before returning to Dunham House," she mused. "It would be nice to see everyone."

"That's settled then," Charles agreed, moving from behind the desk. There was a lot to arrange before they left, starting with convincing Alfred of his plan.

*

Charles found Alfred in the nursery. It was the place he now spent more of his time. Having accepted that he was Frederica's father, he was determined to be the best father he could, which started with learning all there was to know about caring for a child. Charles waited until Alfred gave the baby to the nurse and followed Charles out of the room.

"I wanted to put a proposal to you, which I think you would be interested in," Charles explained as they descended the staircase.

"Go on," Alfred said.

Charles did not continue until they were both in the study and he could close the door, it was not appropriate for the other staff to hear anything at this stage. "I would like to offer you the position of steward at Home Farm," he explained.

"Steward?" Alfred said in surprise. "I don't know the first thing about running an estate."

"No, but Mr Lawson does," Charles responded, amused at Alfred's shocked expression. "I've already taken the liberty of speaking to him about my proposal. He is more than happy to spend the time that you need in order to learn the job. This is a small estate, so the pay is not high, but it does come with accommodation and food, and you can obviously live here with Frederica. Lady Dunham wants someone who will stay and care for the estate, you have already proved yourself to be able and loyal, and I don't think you will have any trouble in learning the role."

Alfred had sat down, leaning forward. He blew air through his teeth, as thoughts raced around his head. "I admit that I was worried about what job I would be able to take with a baby and no mother," he acknowledged.

"The job is only part-time, when you know the ropes," Charles explained. "The staff here are already caring for the baby, there is no reason why that needs to be altered. As she grows you will have more time to spend with her. The only difficulty I can see is the financial side."

Alfred sat straight. "That isn't too much of a concern. I have savings, and Lord Halkyn has provided for Frederica's future, so that is not the worry it might have been. I do not need much to live on."

"Well, it is settled then. I shall write to inform Lord and Lady Dunham," Charles said, happy that his scheme had been so easily accepted.

"Do you not need references? After all, you may know me, but Lord Dunham does not," Alfred said, everything moving a little fast for him.

"He is quick to assess someone, he would not have helped you already if he did not feel that you were worthy. That, along with my recommendation will be enough," Charles assured him. "You will have a lot of hard work over the coming months, it won't be easy initially, especially as Martha and I will be leaving tomorrow."

"Tomorrow?" Alfred asked, surprised for the second time in almost as many minutes. "That's a little sudden isn't it?"

"Yes, but Martha has been notified of a family event that she wishes to attend on the return journey to Dunham House. We have been gone for some time, longer than I think we all had anticipated when we started this journey," Charles acknowledged.

172

"Yes, you have been very accommodating, I never expected so much when I approached Lord Dunham," Alfred said humbly. He knew the Lord and his staff had gone above and beyond anything he had hoped for when he initially approached him. It had been an act of desperation on his part when needing to get Laura to safety.

"Laura did something that deserved help, it was unfair that it ended the way it did. At least this way, there is a small bit of satisfaction at the way events have turned out," Charles said.

"Thank you on behalf of myself and my daughter," Alfred responded with feeling.

*

Martha and Charles left early the following morning. Martha was eager to see her family, as it had been a few years since she had visited and she was keen for the journey to be over. She had been sad to leave Alfred and Frederica, but she knew that they had a life that was now secure.

She lay her head on the padded coach wall of the coach as it left Home Farm behind. "I feel many years older than when I arrived here," she said with a sigh.

"Yes, it hasn't been an easy time for you," Charles responded.

"I think the appropriate response should be 'you don't look a day older, Martha', rather than agreeing with me," Martha could not resist teasing with a smile.

Charles laughed, "You know that I am useless at the flowery language that our betters use."

"Thank goodness," Martha said with feeling. "Some of the nonsense I heard spouted to Lady Dunham before she was married, made my toes curl with embarrassment that the gentleman uttering the words thought it was acceptable to voice such nonsense."

Charles smiled, "My ever practical Martha," he said with affection, "No inane flattery for you."

Martha looked out of the window. She was not the type of woman that wanted false words, but once upon a time she had hoped to meet the man of her dreams, who would sweep her off her feet and look after her, cherish her and love her. How differently life turned out sometimes, and how foolish and naïve were those dreams.

She was roused from her thoughts by Charles, moving his hand and covering hers. "You are not the only one to feel older than when they first came," Charles said quietly, his eyes looking seriously into Martha's. "I still have nightmares about you being hurt, and if I should forget for a few moments, I only need to see your neck to be reminded of how close you were to being lost."

Martha touched the scar on her neck which was disappearing, but had not yet completely vanished. She was a little unsure of what to say to Charles, so just squeezed his hand in return and smiled at him. The Charles she had used to argue with, was far easier to deal with than the Charles that made her insides burn and her mouth dry, robbing her of the use of her brain and ability to form words. That Charles was a far more difficult concept to understand.

Chapter 23

Martha and Charles arrived to a household that was busy with wedding preparations. Martha's mother was even asserting herself and leaving her bedroom, something that she had not done for years. The two youngest boys would not be attending the wedding as they were at sea, but Susan was delighted that her sister had joined the party.

The two sisters slept in the room they had shared since Susan had left the cradle. Martha resumed her duty of brushing out her sister's hair when they retired to bed.

"Your gentleman seems a pleasant man," Martha said, finally glad to be able to speak to her sister alone.

"He is lovely," Susan sighed. "We aren't going to have riches, but I'm sure we are going to be happy."

Martha smiled at her sister, it was obvious that both parties adored each other, they barely looked at anyone else when in each other's company. Martha had only spoken briefly to Mr Horan, her future brother, but he seemed a steady young man. "You don't need riches to be happy, but surely you will be comfortable?" she asked.

"Oh yes," Susan assured her. "Robert is the third son, but his uncle has a title and has promised him a living. He will be a fine clergyman. We hope that one day there may be the opportunity for more than one living, but we are happy to wait."

Martha smiled, Susan was romantic about the whole situation. They might not be so patient if the living was small, but she was not going to spoil her sister's happiness by being the voice of reality. "I'm sure you will be very content and I hope Mr Horan soon receives another living."

"It doesn't matter, I am used to living on virtually nothing," Susan said, with what sounded like a little bitterness. "At least by marrying, I won't need to hand over most of my earnings to Thomas. I don't know how you have done it all these years!"

"Susan!" Martha said shocked. "We are a family, we all need to contribute," she chided her sister.

"Be honest Martha," Susan said, turning to her sister. "Don't you think that Thomas has become a little too accustomed to everyone contributing to his income? Yes, mother costs him sometimes when she needs medication, but she has no other expenses, she never leaves the house and buys no clothing. With the dowry that Alice brought to the marriage and the little income that the land brings, he should not be asking for so much from us."

"It is sometimes difficult, to send so much," Martha acknowledged, remembering how desperate she felt at Thomas's request for her savings.

"Difficult? It has been downright impossible!" Susan exploded. "What is going to happen when we all marry? What will Thomas do then?"

"I don't know," Martha responded, admitting to herself that it was something that she had not considered. There might be no hope that she would marry, but it was highly likely that her brothers would.

"He's changed Martha, you will see for yourself," Susan said.

Martha was to find that Susan was correct, her amiable brother had changed substantially in the years since she had seen him. He constantly spoke about money, no matter who the audience was, something that mortified Martha when Charles was in earshot. Thomas reminded them incessantly of what burdens he had, and of how he had been held back by the actions of their father. By the end of the second day, Martha was ready to scream at him about them all being affected, but she held her counsel. No one would appreciate her spoiling Susan's day, so she gritted her teeth and tried to nod sympathetically.

Susan's wedding day arrived, bright and clear. Martha dressed carefully in a gown, which although it was not her best, (that still being at Dunham House), was acceptable for the occasion. It was a deep peach that was edged in white lace. The colour suited her, it made her look more olive skinned, whereas the same colour may have drained other complexions.

The lace added to the dress' elegance, rather than adding edging for the sake of it. Susan had insisted on dressing Martha's hair, making it into a softer style than the practical one she usually wore.

Martha followed the bride down the aisle, acting as a maid of honour. Susan had dressed in a cream gown, with lilac flowers. Charles stood in one of the pews with the other guests, but if questioned could not have described the bride's apparel. He was too busy staring at the maid of honour, to notice anything else.

Martha glowed as she walked down the aisle. She looked younger and softer than she did in her work dresses, with a tight bun on the top of her head. Although Charles had always thought her striking, he thought she was stunning as she smiled at him, when she caught his eye. She blushed a little, which made something inside of him curl. He wanted to jump over the pews and push the bride and groom out of the way, forcing the clergyman to marry the two of them instead. How he wished at that moment, in addition to many others, that she had taken his proposal in the spirit he had offered it.

The wedding breakfast went off without a hitch and the bride and groom took their leave. They were to take a short break in Wales before moving in to their vicarage. The guests waved off the carriage, before returning to the house.

Martha noticed that her mother was no longer looking as well as she had done throughout the morning and approached her. "Mama, do you need to rest?" she asked gently, in order not to bring any attention to them both.

"I need to return to my bedchamber, I can feel the start of something coming on," came the pained voice that Martha was familiar with.

"Perhaps it will not take hold," Martha said, trying to be positive and rouse her parent from accepting that she was heading into a decline. "You have looked so well these last few days."

"I did not want to worry Susan," came the self-pitying reply. "I need to see the apothecary, I need some medication. Can you ask Thomas to send for him? Mr Wood always knows what I need."

Martha assured her mother that she would ask her brother to send for the apothecary and helped her into bed. She suspected that being an invalid was now more of a habit than anything else, because she had looked so healthy during the run up to the wedding and been as involved as any of them had been. Martha was not sure of what the solution was, but approached the drawing room to speak to her brother with trepidation.

The guests had left by the time Martha returned. Thomas was sitting with his wife, Alice, eating some of the fancies that were left over from the breakfast. Martha cleared her throat.

"Thomas, Mother is asking for the apothecary to be sent for," she started.

"She usually wants him after exerting herself," Alice said with a sigh.

"I'm sure there is still some medication left from last time, ask her maid to give her that," Thomas said with a dismissive wave of his hand. "She will soon stop asking for him."

"How often does he visit?" Martha asked.

"I've started just requesting the medication, it's cheaper that way," Thomas responded. "Which brings me on to your contributions," he said, looking at Martha.

"What about them?" Martha asked stiffly. She had to admit to understanding Susan's bitterness when looking at the standard of living that Thomas and Alice shared. Even taking into account the burden of their mother on their finances, they lived very well.

"Susan is refusing to pay any more towards the upkeep of her home," Thomas said with disgust.

"She is married now!" Martha exclaimed. "This is no longer her home and she can hardly ask her husband to support this house, when they will have very little to live on themselves." Martha was astounded that her brother would even contemplate such a thing. Susan had been correct, he had changed beyond all recognition. Where was the brother who was concerned about condemning his sisters to a life in service? It was as if he had never existed, when looking at the man sat before her.

"There are only the two of them, they can live very cheaply," Thomas snapped.

"And there are only the three of you," Martha snapped back. "And I seem to recall that Alice brought with her a dowry, while Susan has not had that benefit."

"Anyway, we are digressing," Thomas said, with yet another dismissive wave of his hand. A habit that Martha was beginning to detest. "Because of Susan's refusal to continue to support us, I shall need you to increase your contributions," he said without a flicker of embarrassment or shame.

Martha stared at her brother in disbelief, "You cannot be serious, surely?"

"Why not? We need a certain level of income. You are earning, therefore you need to provide more," Thomas said, choosing another fancy. He was acting as it was as if his request was perfectly reasonable.

"Thomas I cannot afford to send any more money," Martha said, quietly, but firmly.

"You must," Thomas insisted. "Why can you not afford it? What else has a woman like you to spend her money on?"

Martha looked at her brother, tears springing to her eyes. She should be stronger than to have such an extreme reaction to an unkind remark, but whether it was because she had been involved in a wedding, or whether part of her recognised herself all too clearly in Thomas's words, she did not know. Her instinct was to flee the room and never see her brother again, but of course she could not act so hysterically. So, she sat, trying to fight the overwhelming sadness that threatened to drown her that Thomas's words had caused.

Just as she was about to try and respond to the question, she heard a noise from the door and turned to see Charles walking into the room, with a look of anger on his face the likes she had never seen before.

Charles strode over to Thomas and punched him squarely on the jaw before the other man knew what was happening, let alone what had hit him. Sugar fancies and china plates scattered across the room, as Thomas fell backwards, kicking the occasional table with his feet, as they left the floor.

"Don't you ever speak to your sister, the one who has stood by you more than any other person would ever have done, in such a way again. The next time I hear anything like that uttered from your mouth, it won't just be one punch I issue. Do I make myself clear?" Charles snarled at Thomas, standing over him, like an animal ready to pounce. Anger was pulsing from his body as he waited for Thomas's response. "Well? Are you only brave in front of someone who is more disadvantaged than you are? I would hate to see how you treat your tenants, you are nothing but a coward, living off the spoils of others."

"Charles!" Martha exclaimed, her heart was pounding at the sight of Charles coming to her defence in such a way, but she automatically tried to defend her brother.

"He has used you for the last time Martha," Charles said, without looking at her. He was focused too closely on her brother, almost willing him to say the wrong thing again.

Thomas looked at the man stood over him, while he rubbed his jaw. Charles had guessed right in that Thomas was a coward, but he was in his own house, which gave him some confidence, as all the staff would do as he bid. He struggled to stand, but then tried to square up to Charles, the action did not quite work, as Charles was athletic, trim and fuelled by righteous anger, whilst Thomas was rotund, smaller and not quite able to look at the indignant man with conviction.

"How dare you come into my home and attack me like this!" he spat at Charles. "I will be sending for the magistrate unless you leave immediately."

"I am leaving, not because of your threat, but because I cannot stand to be in the company of such a parasite," Charles hissed, his face going close to Thomas's, causing the smaller man to take a step backwards. "I imagine that if your accounts were examined, we would find one of two things. That either you are a man overspending at every opportunity, or even worse, you have a substantial nest egg that has been obtained by draining your sibling's resources."

Martha could not believe Charles's audacity, and was just about to step in and stop the situation from deteriorating further when she saw Thomas colour at the second accusation and she suddenly felt very, very sick.

Charles had also noticed the change in Thomas. "So, you have been taking money off them at every opportunity and feathering your own nest? You are worse than I thought." Charles stepped back shaking his head, he did not want to touch the man before him again. The thought of what worry and hardship he had caused Martha was making him want to forego all reason and find something to pummel the man until he could do no more harm.

"Thomas?" Martha asked, finally able to speak without tasting the bile that had threatened to rise at the realisation of what her brother had done.

"What?" Thomas snapped. "Oh, I see you looking at me as if I'm in the wrong! Well before you condemn me, just think what I have had to put up with all these years."

"I know selling the land and making the remainder profitable must have been hard," Martha acknowledged, always fair. "But surely, once you started to make a profit, we could have stopped our contributions?"

"Oh yes, you would have all liked that wouldn't you?" Thomas snarled. "Leave me here to look after Mother and you all go off into the world without a care in the world! Do you know what it's like living here with her? 'Oh, I need this, oh, I need that, more medicine, Thomas!' Day in, day out, it's enough to drive anyone insane!"

Martha stared at her brother in disbelief. She no longer knew the man before her and more importantly, no longer wanted to know him. "I cannot believe that you have said that we have gone off without a care in the world! Do you have any idea what it is like being in service Thomas? Getting up day after day, knowing that the only time it will end is when you are too old to do it anymore, and hoping against hope that your employer will offer some cottage or room that you can afford to rent until the end. Do you know how insecure that future is Thomas?"

"It all sounds very dramatic," Thomas responded with derision.

Martha had seen Charles move, but placed her hand on his arm, this was her argument. "It is uneventful, rather than dramatic Thomas, I suggest you take some of my hard earned money that you have stashed away and take yourself off to the theatre, in order to experience real drama. I shall take my leave from you and shall not be returning. I suggest you also use your nest egg to pay for mother's medication in the future, as there will be no other communication from me, monetary or other."

"You have responsibilities here, you can't stop sending money," Thomas demanded, refusing to admit defeat.

"I can and I will," Martha said, standing. "I have given more than enough, including my retirement money, and you will not receive another farthing from me, Thomas! I shall also be writing to our brothers and informing them of what I am doing. I wouldn't want you writing to them and accusing me of falsehoods, now would I?"

Thomas lunged at his sister, the thought of losing all the income from all of his siblings too much to bear. Before he reached Martha, he was knocked out of the way by Charles, who bodily charged him.

"If you ever try to lay a finger on your sister again, I will kill you, do I make myself clear?" Charles snarled at Thomas.

"Get out!" Thomas hissed, once again on the floor in his own drawing room.

"Don't worry, we are going, I dislike the company in this part of the world," Charles said, offering his arm to Martha.

They walked through the door and Charles closed it firmly behind him. He gave orders for their bags to be packed immediately and for the carriage to be brought around. Martha did not say a word, but Charles could feel her trembling against his arm. She attempted to remove her hand from him, her sense of propriety overriding her need to feel his strength, but he placed his hand over hers, holding it firmly, but gently on his arm.

Charles and Martha remained in the hallway until the carriage was brought round and then they alighted. Martha had made no further attempt to be separated from Charles, not even to take leave of her mother. She had felt that if she left the warmth of Charles's hand, she would collapse in a heap and not have the strength to ever stand again. She had only tried to remove her hand because she felt that she ought to do so, but the relief that had washed over her when he placed his hand over hers had almost overwhelmed her, finding that she was grateful for his support.

The carriage finally set off, Martha did not look back at her home. She sat stiffly, looking forward, not really seeing anything and trying to stop herself from feeling as if she was rudderless and adrift.

Chapter 24

Charles let Martha be during the day, he realised what a shock Thomas's revelation and behaviour had been. He had rarely felt so angry, he had wanted to inflict real harm on Thomas from the moment he had heard his callous words. He should not have listened at the doorway, he had not intended doing so, but he had instantly wanted to support Martha and could not walk away. When Thomas's words had demeaned Martha in such a way, he had acted without thinking, wanting to inflict pain on the person who had caused pain to the one he cared about.

He cursed himself silently. Martha would probably take him to task when she thought about what he had done. He had acted like a possessive child, but that was how she made him feel, not so much like the child, but far too possessive for his own comfort. He knew that he had no right to those feelings and that she would not welcome his interference, but he could not have stood by and seen her hurt, without doing something. Perhaps knocking her brother to the ground twice was not the best thing to have done though. She would never consider him a gentleman.

They travelled in almost total silence, only communicating when it was necessary. Martha felt drained, but having Charles with her was comforting. He did not demand any explanations and she was grateful for his tact.

They eventually stopped at an inn for the evening and after eating a small meal, Martha retired to her bedchamber. She was not sure if she would sleep, but she needed to be alone. She had intended writing to her brothers, but sat in front of a small table, with paper and quill, but unable to write the words.

A gentle knock at the door disturbed Martha from her reverie. She opened the door slightly, to reveal a troubled looking Charles.

"May I come in?" Charles asked quietly. Although they were in an inn, miles away from anyone who knew them, it was not appropriate for him to be asking for admittance to an unmarried lady's bed chamber.

Martha moved aside and allowed Charles to enter. "Is there anything amiss?" she asked.

"I cannot sleep until I apologise," Charles started, walking over to the fireplace and turning to face Martha.

"Whatever for?" Martha asked, surprised.

"I should never have behaved in such a way, especially in your brother's house. I'm sorry Martha," Charles said, his words rushing out, needing to have it confirmed that he had completely lost any hope of securing her affection. He had convinced himself that once he heard her disgust at his actions, he would be able to accept that he had lost whatever sliver of hope he had and he would try to let go of her.

"There is no need to apologise," Martha said quietly.

"I acted like a brute, without sense or decorum," Charles continued, giving her the words he had expected to hear.

"I'm glad you did," Martha responded, not quite meeting his gaze.

It took a moment or two for Martha's words to sink in, but once they had Charles needed them confirming. "You are glad I acted as if I was in a tavern brawl?" he asked in disbelief.

"During the carriage ride, I thought that I have never had anyone coming to my rescue, as you did today," Martha started, flushing. "But then I remembered that I have."

Charles did not realise stomachs could plummet into one's boots until he heard those words. "Who was it?" he asked, but his voice had dulled.

"You know him," Martha said, with the first smile of the day. "He was the one that promised that he would bring Elizabeth back to me safe and sound, he was the one who cared for me when Laura had been attacked and he was the one that today stood up against my cheating brother and gave me the strength to stand up for myself."

"Martha, I...." Charles started, not sure of how to express himself, but Martha stopped him, by placing her hand on his arm.

"I own that when we first met, I disliked you, perhaps it was insecurity, perhaps jealousy, perhaps even attraction," Martha admitted, flushing a deep red. "But it was not very long before I realised that I had done you a disservice and I did not know how to right it. I'm sorry Charles, I am ashamed of how I have behaved."

"But you said no when I asked you to marry me," Charles said, struggling to keep himself under control. He had the feeling that this was a one and only chance to make things right and he was determined to make every word count.

"I thought it was a proposal made out of pity and I did not want to trap you into a marriage that you would regret. Perhaps there was some wounded pride at play too," Martha responded, looking down with embarrassment at admitting so much.

"Oh Martha, do you not know me well enough to know that I would never have made such a proposal out of pity?" Charles asked exasperated.

"It was after Thomas's request for money, so I thought it must be," Martha responded honestly.

"It gave me the perfect excuse, to utter the words that I'd wanted to say for a long time, but I had guessed that you would not welcome me declaring myself like a love sick fool. It wasn't the best time to make the proposal, I realised that almost as soon as I'd said the words, but they were there, inside me, wanting to come out," Charles said with a shrug.

"Like a love sick fool?" Martha asked.

Charles took hold of Martha's hands and held her at arm's length, he still was not sure if she would push him away if he tried to hold her closer. "Have I not been completely transparent?" he asked. "I have thought that I was constantly revealing how smitten I've been for so long now, that I cannot remember when it started, but it was probably the day I first met you."

"But you tormented me," Martha said, thinking back over the times that he had angered her.

"I did not know how to act, you appeared so far above me in every respect," Charles admitted. "At first, I wanted to see if I could get beyond that cool, calm exterior. Another man would have achieved it through poetry and words, but not me. No, I went blundering in, and instead of making you fall into my arms, you hated me."

"I didn't hate you, never that, but I was so angry," Martha admitted.

"When I realised what I had done, it was too late," Charles continued. "I have only ever wanted you to be mine."

"Oh."

Charles sighed, this was not looking good. "Oh?" he asked. "Am I too late then? Are you going to turn me away again when I ask you to be my wife for the second time?"

Martha's eyes filled with tears, she had to ask the next question and although she wanted the truth, she dreaded the response. "Be honest with me, please. Are you asking out of pity after what has happened today?"

Charles squeezed her hands. "I once asked you to trust me and you said that you did," he started, looking her directly in the face. "Do you still trust me?"

"Yes," Martha responded, feeling breathless all of a sudden.

"Good," Charles replied with feeling. "I want to marry you because you drive me to distraction, because I want to be the one who you drape your hair over while you sleep, because I love you and not through pity, but because you are a beautiful, vibrant, capable woman, who I would be proud of to call my wife."

Martha took a deep breath and a slow smile spread across her face. "In that case, I suppose I should say yes." Her laugh was lost as Charles pulled her towards him and kissed her, not gently as he had intended, but fully, forcefully, the kiss of a man in love, who had waited too long.

Martha responded to her man. Yes, her man, by wrapping her arms around his neck and pulling him close. The day that had seemed to end so badly, had ended in the best way possible. Charles loved her, he actually loved her and she loved him. She had admitted it to herself, but being able to acknowledge it openly and tell him again and again, made her feel lightheaded.

Charles took pleasure in the woman in his arms, who was responding to him as she had never responded before. Every time he thought that he was pushing her too far, she responded with a small moan and held him closer, encouraging him further.

He forced himself to pull back and although he cupped her cheek in his hand, he stopped kissing her. "We need to marry soon," he said, taking deep breaths in an effort to control himself. "I can't be responsible for my actions if we are forced to have a long engagement."

Martha smiled, "We are too old for long engagements."

"Speak for yourself, there is life in this old dog yet," Charles said, nipping her bottom lip with his teeth.

Martha moaned softly. "How soon were you thinking?"

"Special licence?" Charles asked.

"Definitely," Martha agreed, trying to kiss Charles. She felt as if they had talked for long enough.

"Martha, stop," Charles groaned, returning the kisses, but trying to keep control, not easy when the love of your life, was being as tempting as Martha was. "If we continue…."

"Yes?" Martha asked.

Charles pulled away again, "Martha, there comes a point when a man's resolve disappears and there is no turning back. I am reaching that point, I need to leave before you force every rational thought from my mind."

"I had hoped that you were already beyond that point," Martha said provocatively, but the words caused her to blush, showing her innocence.

Charles almost sank to his knees with the effort of keeping his actions under control. "Martha, you don't realise what your words mean. If I stay…"

"I want you to stay, I know what my words mean," Martha said quietly. "We have both been foolish, I don't want to be apart from you another moment."

"Oh God, Martha, I love you," Charles said, picking her up in one easy movement. He walked over to the bed and laid her down gently. "We will never be apart again."

Epilogue

Alfred became an efficient steward, as Charles had anticipated. He took on the role seriously and worked hard to ensure that Home Farm was as efficient as it could be. He instilled loyalty in the small staff that worked in the house and the tenant farmers that worked on the land.

He did not marry until Frederica was fully grown. Being the steady man that he was, he took his commitment to his daughter as seriously as he took every other task he took on. Frederica grew up, secure that she was loved and although knowing that her father had loved her mother, she was not told of the history that brought her parents together. When she married a local farmer, she was delighted when her father married the maid who had cared for her throughout her life. The young maid had become her substitute mother and for Frederica it was perfect that the two people whom she loved as much as she did her husband, should find happiness together. Lord and Lady Halkyn took a keen interest in Frederica throughout her life and provided her with opportunities that she would not have normally had, which enriched her upbringing even more.

Alfred loved Laura until his dying day, but he was able to open his heart eventually to another love and was loved in return. He had no other children, but he found contentment with his wife and they both indulged their grandchildren as they increased the size of their family.

Charles and Martha returned to Dunham House and were married soon afterwards. Charles insisted that he wrote to Martha's brother and although Martha had no idea what had been written in the letter, a few weeks later she received a letter of apology from her brother containing the money she had set aside for her retirement. Charles and Martha never mentioned the incident again and although Martha kept in touch with her family, she could never quite feel the same about her eldest brother.

They had two children, which was a double blessing, as Martha had presumed that her age would prevent her from having children at all.

Charles had to endure two occasions when he prowled the house, as expectant fathers had done before him, while his wife was in labour. Two boys filled the house which had become their home on the Dunham Estate. Martha never tired of the noise, mess or tricks that her boys created. She was also able to provide a second home to the children of Lord and Lady Dunham, who visited on a daily basis, enjoying being in such a welcoming home.

Lady Dunham had been delighted that Martha had found happiness, but experienced a real wrench that the woman who had been her companion and friend for so many years, was no longer living under the same roof. Not one for visiting normally, there were few days that passed without Lady Dunham walking down to Martha's cottage with her children and sitting down at the kitchen table, gossiping and chatting.

Every morning Charles awoke with a silent prayer of thanks. His Martha was not the prim and proper woman that he had first met. She was vibrant, passionate and challenged him whenever she disagreed with him, which unfortunately for him, was often. Luckily for Charles, he could always bring a smile to Martha's lips when he took her into his arms and reminded her exactly why she had agreed to marry him.

Martha was finally living the life she had thought was out of her reach and had never been happier.

About the Author

Audrey Harrison has always wanted to write, or live in the Regency period, but life, work and problems with time travel stopped her. Anyway, circumstances change and the dream began! (Well, maybe not the travel back to the Regency period, but I would not admit to that anyway, would I?)

The Complicated Earl and the Reluctant Earl have proved really popular and the modern take on a regency novel, A Very Modern Lord has also done really well.

When writing An Inconvenient Ward, it was going to be a stand-alone book, but as the story progressed, so did the sub stories. There is now a trilogy to the series, An Inconvenient Ward, An Inconvenient Wife and An Inconvenient Companion. Each book can be read alone, but I hope that readers enjoy finding out about the other characters in the stories.

If you enjoy the books, please would you take the time to write a review on Amazon? Reviews are vital for an author who is just starting out, although I admit to bad ones being crushing. Selfishly, I want readers to love my characters just as much as I do!

I can be contacted for any comments you may have, via my website

www.audreyharrison.co.uk

www.facebook.com/AudreyHarrisonAuthor

Thank you for your support and for your enjoyment, please find Chapter One of An Inconvenient Ward, the first book of the series.

Chapter 1

London. January 1815

Lord Dunham was bored. In fact he was bored, bored, bored. He looked at his reflection in the full length cheval mirror, as he struggled to fix his cravat. Normally this task would not be the ordeal that it had turned into today, so much so that his valet had wisely retreated to the rear of the large bed chamber. He watched in mortification as his master ruined one cravat after another as the struggle to tie one to his satisfaction continued. The pile of creased cravats on the bed mounted, and the sighs and curses increased equally as fast as Lord Dunham reached the end of his tether with his neckwear.

Michael paused and stared at the face looking back at him in the mirror. When had he lost his spark? He had until four years ago been plain Mr Michael Birchall. He was heir to the then Lord Dunham and in fact had been named after him in honour of the family connection. He had not seen much of Uncle Michael as he had grown up, knowing him only as a figure in the background who took a general, but distant, interest in his heir. Everyone, including the young Michael, had presumed Lord Dunham would marry, and produce his own heir and thus he would be disinherited. The expectation had not upset the young man, he refused to miss what he had never had, and he enjoyed the life he had been born to, to the full.

He had spent his formative years in the country. His father was Lord Dunham's younger brother. He had married young, but an illness of the brain had prevented him taking part in family life. No one spoke about the illness; everyone was reluctant to acknowledge that there was madness in the family. Fortunately, his living in the country enabled such an affliction to be ignored by most of their society.

Michael had an older sister Violet, and, between his sister and mother, he had enjoyed a childhood knowing that he was loved. Once old enough, even though he may have been considered young by an outsider, Michael ran the estate in place of his father, due to his father's illness. He became master in his own right when he inherited the estate after his father's death. Michael had had to learn to deal in a matter of fact way with such a curse in his family.

His mother had passed away peacefully when he was in his late teens and he had mourned her loss, but he still had Violet, and the affection between brother and sister increased as their family became smaller. Violet had eventually married a good man, Edward Parker, whom Michael was happy to call brother, and she quickly produced three girls. Michael constantly teased her about needing to provide him with an heir, but she was content with her darlings. Her girls were showered with the same affection that Michael and Violet had been shown as children. She was a natural mother and the most important person in Michael's life.

When Michael had come of age he had spent his time in the London Season and had enjoyed himself to the full. He was not seen as a great heir; Lord Dunham's health was good and he was still seen as a good catch by many of the ladies, even some of the younger ones. Desire for a fortune often overcame any reserves that marrying a substantially older man might have caused. So Michael was able to enjoy the entertainments and parties without having any fortune hunters having him in their sights. There was no pressure on him and he took full benefit of the lack of restrictions.

Lord Dunham financed Michael's Grand Tour and ensured that he was accompanied by a tutor who would instil the ways of a gentleman. So Michael learned and developed on the Continent, returning a finer gentleman than before. His return to London saw him conquer a few more hearts, but never seriously fall in love. He was having too much fun to settle down. If he yearned for family life he spent time with Violet, Edward and their brood.

The week after Michael's twenty-fourth birthday, his life changed forever. A sudden, unexpected seizure caused Lord Dunham to pass away, long before anyone had anticipated. Michael was no longer just plain Mr Birchall, but the new Lord Dunham. Those who had previously dismissed him as a gentleman of no real importance suddenly wanted to become his friend. His good looks and manners had always made him popular with the ladies, but he now became so popular that he felt hunted.

He was now twenty-eight. Four long years had passed since he had enjoyed a carefree lifestyle. Most days it felt as if decades had passed. At times like today when he really studied his reflection in his looking glass, he hardly recognised the man he had become.

No-one could accuse him of being unattractive; his dark, slightly curly hair fell naturally in all the latest fashions. His skin was pale and unblemished, and his eyes were a deep brown that seemed to reflect his very soul when they were not guarded. Nowadays, only Violet saw them sparkle with laughter or warm with feeling; most of his friends or acquaintances saw the closed expression of a man keeping his distance. Little did they know that part of that reserve was caused by the fear that he would suffer the same fate as his father had. Once madness was in a family, all of its members feared contamination. Every new emotion was examined by Michael to see if it was a sign that the illness had started.

He had taken to managing his new estates seriously. He had had a lot to learn and when he had seen what his life would be once he had inherited the title, he had preferred to immerse himself in learning everything he needed to know about estate management on a huge scale. He had a large estate in Somerset, tucked away but still convenient, as it was within easy reach of Bath. It was the Dunham principal home and was a beautiful Jacobean building that rambled over three floors. Michael had continued the improvements that had been planned, and anyone lucky enough to visit commented that although the property was grand in appearance it was also a comfortable, welcoming home.

A house in Belgrave Square and a hunting lodge in Leicester completed his property portfolio and gave him enough escape to maintain his sanity. Michael had enjoyed the London life as a gentleman about town, but once he had discovered just how little he enjoyed the fickleness that a title attracted, he very often escaped to Somerset, or to Violet's home in Hampshire. Sometimes, though, he was forced to come to London and this was where he found himself now. Forced to spend the Season in

London because of an agreement his uncle had made years ago. It was this that had put him in the foulest mood he had experienced for a long time. Finally, with a sigh, he accepted that he could not put off the morning any longer and went to greet his solicitor, leaving his valet to mourn over the destruction of so many freshly starched cravats.

Michael entered his library, usually a place he enjoyed spending time, but it offered no pleasure on this morning. He greeted his solicitor in his usual brusque way. "Have you managed to find a way out of this mess for me? Any last minute miracles that will spare me spending the Season in this godforsaken place?" They were the same questions he had been asking over the last few months.

"No, your Lordship, the agreement is immutable; there is no way out of it. The only advantage is that it will last a lot less than a year."

"From my perspective, that is still an inordinate amount of time ahead of me!" came the disparaging reply.

The solicitor was enjoying this meeting as little as Lord Dunham, and answered a quiet, "Quite so." The quicker all the details could be finally agreed on, the quicker he could return to the sanctity of his office and leave his Lordship to deal with the situation as he chose.

A few moments later the silence was interrupted by the butler who announced a Miss Elizabeth Rufford and Miss Martha Fairfield. Michael had moved forward slightly to greet the newcomers, but the sight before him stopped him in his tracks. Miss Fairfield was obviously a governess or something similar. She was around thirty, dressed in the grey high-necked dress that was the accepted uniform of a governess, finished with a shawl and bonnet. She had a pleasant face and was as presentable as most of her supposed profession were; the sight that had stopped Michael was Miss Elizabeth Rufford.

Bounding into the room was a vision of purple and orange ruffles and feathers. He had never seen anything like it before in his life. Her dress was of the brightest purple and edged in bright orange ribbons and frills.

The hat she wore looked too big and had huge purple and orange feathers coming out of every possible surface. Michael could hardly see the person underneath for the curling feathers. The lady's figure he could not judge because of the amount of frills and ruffles that surrounded her and he could see no hair from underneath the bonnet. No ringlets framed the lady's face as was the custom, not a hair was visible and for a split second Michael wondered if she was bald. The only redeeming feature was her eyes; they were hazel in colour and sparkled with laughter as she took in the astonishment of the two gentlemen who stood before her.

"Good morning gentlemen, I hope you are well. When will his Lordship be joining us? I hope he is of a strong constitution!" She laughed and Michael wondered how it was possible that her eyes seemed to sparkle even more.

The solicitor started to speak, but Michael cut him off with a glare. He bowed in greeting, but instead of introducing himself he started with a question. "Why does Lord Dunham need to have a strong constitution?" He asked curiously.

"Well actually I hope he doesn't," she answered frankly, but with a mischievous smile. "I'm hoping that one look at me will give him a heart attack and then this silly ward thing will be at an end before it has started."

Michael raised his eyebrows and said with a drawl. "A little harsh, I think Miss Rufford, wishing to murder your guardian."

"I don't wish to murder him. I just want to release us both from this nonsense."

"His Lordship wishes release as much as you appear to do, I assure you." Michael responded drily, but with feeling.

"Oh, does he? That's excellent. I thought he might be one who would try and dictate how I should live my life and how I should act. I never wanted a guardian!" she responded.

"I can assure you that your guardian never wanted a ward." Michael responded with a shudder.

"My Lord, if you please..." the solicitor interrupted, looking uncomfortable.

Michael sighed. "Miss Rufford, my solicitor seems determined to spoil the sliver of fun in this otherwise extremely tedious day. Please let me introduce my solicitor Mr Hammond, and please allow me to introduce myself, Lord Dunham. I am at your service madam." Michael finished the introduction with a flourishing bow that any dandy would be proud of.

Elizabeth's eyes opened wide, she looked from one to the other as if waiting for them to announce that it was a joke. Seeing the expressions on their faces she realised that they were serious. "But you are not old!" she exclaimed, finally accepting that she really was faced with the real Lord Dunham.

"Thank you for the compliment, Miss Rufford," Michael responded coolly. "I don't consider myself to be in my dotage quite yet."

"How can you be my guardian? You cannot have studied with my father when the agreement was made. This must be wrong!" Elizabeth's sparkling eyes had been replaced with eyes that flashed with frustration, something which amused Michael. It was some comfort to know that he was no longer the only one suffering because of the situation.

"I can confirm that I did not study with your father. My uncle, the previous Lord Dunham, was your father's friend, and he was the one who made the agreement. Unfortunately for us both I have the same name as my uncle, Michael Thomas George Birchall, Lord Dunham. Your father's will did not specify which Lord Dunham, just the full name, which I share. Believe me, I have had the legalities checked and double checked. Until your twenty-first birthday, I am your guardian." Michael spoke as if the whole situation bored him.

"Well that changes everything!" Elizabeth responded after taking a moment or two to absorb the information. "It looks like you have been travelling with a grotesque monster for nothing, Martha." Elizabeth had turned to her companion and smiled apologetically. She took off the hat and threw it down on a seat. "I'm glad to take that thing off; you would not believe the stares I have received whilst wearing it."

"Oh I think I would Miss Rufford." Michael replied with a raise of an eyebrow.

Elizabeth laughed. "All that planning for nothing! Oh damn and blast! What am I going to do now?"

Michael was intrigued by the woman seated before him. He had not known what to expect, but she was proving to be more interesting than he had imagined. She had recovered from news that would have mortified any other lady of his acquaintance and instead of swooning away, had cursed as any man would have done. He still was not happy with the situation and needed to draw things together further so they could be efficiently and quickly sorted out. The less time he needed to spend acting as a guardian the better.

"Would you like to accompany me to the drawing room? We can take some refreshments and discuss what you are going to do while in London."

He rang for tea and led the way into his drawing room. It was a large square room with two large windows, facing onto the street and allowing in as much light as possible. The fireplace was marble and Adams styled, with two pillars at each side of the fireplace. The mantelpiece was decorated with a central urn and with the characteristic vines stretching out across the marble, it was simple, but stylish. Blue and gold patterned wallpaper adorned the walls with matching material covering the sofas and chairs, and the curtains were of a shimmering gold, bringing out the gold in the furnishings. The room was grand, but so understated that it managed to have a light airy feel to it.

"Oh what a lovely room!" Elizabeth exclaimed, as she sat in one of the chairs. She ran her hand appreciatively down one of the chair arms, the material felt thick and silky to the touch. "The colours are beautiful. Did your wife choose them?"

"I am not married, and am quite capable of choosing decoration myself." Michael responded a little harshly, indicating that Miss Fairfield should be seated, before he sat himself in a fireside chair.

"It seems a shame to let me into this room dressed as I am. I must clash terribly!" Elizabeth said with a twinkle in her eyes, but she tried to look remorseful.

"You do." came the unkind reply. Michael was in no mood to offer empty flattery to the woman before him.

If Michael had expected Elizabeth to be daunted by his manner he was mistaken, she just threw her head back and laughed. "I know! It's terrible isn't it? The problem is all my clothes are like this, my purpose was to scare my guardian into sending me away."

"You are doing an excellent job of achieving your aim Miss Rufford," Michael said with a shudder. "I dread to think why you wanted to appear as you have."

Elizabeth started fiddling with her hair as she spoke. "I will be honest with you my Lord; I don't want to be in London for the Season. I would much rather be allowed to live in the country running an estate, and enjoying myself, rather than being forced to be someone I am not while supposedly looking for a husband." While talking she had released her hair and shook it out.

Miss Fairfield protested at the action, "Elizabeth please, you should not be attending to your toilette in his Lordship's drawing room."

Elizabeth waved Miss Fairfield's words away and scooped her long dark wavy hair into a loose bun. "Don't worry yourself Martha, his Lordship won't mind me making myself slightly more presentable, I'm sure." Wisps of hair fell out at the sides, which was far more flattering than the harsh bun that had originally been hidden under her hat.

Michael was intrigued. "If you do not wish to have a Season in London, why on earth have you travelled all the way from Lancashire?"

Elizabeth sighed, the first sign of anything but mischievous good humour since she had walked in. "When Papa died three years ago his title, like yours, went to a nephew, Mr Herbert Rufford. I didn't object or feel aggrieved, as I knew my cousin a little and we had got on well when we were young. He did not want to settle in Lancashire so continued enjoying his life travelling between London and Brighton. He did spend *some* time on the estate, but I was unofficially in charge. I make a good estate manager!" She said defensively when Michael had looked at her with disbelief.

"I never said a word." Michael said, amused at the outburst his sceptical expression had caused.

Elizabeth looked as if she did not believe that Michael was not mocking her. "I ran the estate before Papa's death. He would have preferred to have had a boy and treated me more like one while he was alive. Poor Papa, he never remarried after mother died, so he was destined to be disappointed, by just having me."

She said her words in such a matter of fact way that Michael had to admire her stoicism. He had grown up being secure in his relative's affections, even through his father's illness, and had never felt the effects of someone being disappointed with him. Something bordering on compassion stirred in him, but he quickly dismissed it, and carried on listening to her story.

"I'm sure he appreciated you in his own way." he said, an uncommonly reassuring comment from the distant Lord Dunham.

"Possibly, but I will never truly know," came the candid reply. "When I reached the age that I should have come out, I noticed that Papa did not seem to be in his usual good health. I begged him not to bring me to London that year. It did not matter about putting my Season off, as I didn't want to come anyway. Having a Season has never really appealed to me. As it happened it was fortunate we did not travel, Papa deteriorated and was ill for months before he passed away. I am forever thankful that he died at home, not in some damp lodging house in London."

"Why did you not come to London after your period of mourning?" Michael had only heard of the agreement a few months prior, but he had been informed that Elizabeth's father had died over three years ago.

"When it became apparent that Herbert did not want to manage the estate I offered to do it for him. I'm far cheaper than employing an official estate manager so it was an offer he would have been a fool to refuse. It suited me too, it meant that I could put off going to London indefinitely and still live in the area I loved. I knew Herbert would marry one day, but when I did meet his new wife I realised almost immediately what would happen."

"Did she resent your presence?"

"Yes, how did you guess?" Elizabeth smiled ruefully. "At first I had thought that things would go on as normal, but I had not taken Miranda into account. Miranda! I mean to say, what sort of a name is Miranda? It's a doll's name! Believe me, she may have looked like a doll with her golden curls and blue eyes, but she had the viciousness of a cat when moving in for the kill. She saw me as a threat even though I had made the estate extremely profitable. I had to go and that was that."

"As simple as that?" Michael asked, a little admiring of the woman who had taken on this energetic creature sitting before him.

"Yes. She had the perfect get out clause didn't she? I had a guardian who was responsible for me and I had never had a Season in London. As she put it, *even* someone like me should be able to attract some sort of husband; after all, I have my two thousand a year. She informed me that men would put up with anything for that amount of money. So here I am." Elizabeth shrugged with her final words.

Michael had detected no bitterness, but some hurt in the words, and again he felt a little compassion for Elizabeth. It was not her fault that she was not wanted by her family. This type of situation happened regularly and the wardship was not her doing. "So are you looking for a husband?" Two thousand a year would guarantee that she would receive many offers of marriage, even dressed as she was at the moment.

"I was hoping to persuade my guardian to let me establish myself somewhere in the country," Elizabeth explained. "I don't know the ways of society; I have never lived in it. I am happier in the countryside. I could buy a farm and run it myself, I would be self-sufficient and no trouble to anyone."

"That would be seen as quite eccentric." For some reason Michael did not want her ridiculed by society, but that would be guaranteed if she mentioned in wider society, ideas such as running her own estate.

"Who would I be harming?" Elizabeth asked, looking at him candidly.

"No one, in truth." Michael admitted reluctantly.

"Will you help me then?" She asked hopefully.

Michael thought carefully. In many respects it would be the perfect solution, and the easy way out of her being his ward. He would not have to do more than help her find an estate and then make sure things were in place, perhaps to offer support if she needed it. He could then return to his life as it had been before he had been told of his burden.

Something held him back though, whether it was the sparkle that he had seen in her eyes that had drawn him to her initially, he did not know. It could have been the hurt in her voice when she had referred to what had been said about her lack of ability to attract a husband, which had struck something deep within him. He had felt the stirrings of something he did not recognise, all he knew was that he wanted to make things better for her.

He knew how it was to feel that you were just being courted for your fortune. Many Society families would have been reluctant to link to his family because of his father's illness, but once the fortune was in place, anything, even madness, could be overlooked. He had known what it was like to enjoy London though. It had been a pleasant experience sometimes. He could hardly believe his own mind when he became convinced that perhaps she should stay after all.

"I will help you." he finally said.

"Oh good. I have heard of an estate in Yorkshire, it is known locally as Home Farm. It is in need of a lot of work, but it means that I could afford to buy it. It would be hard for the first few years, but I am convinced I could turn it around and make it profitable." Elizabeth babbled, the relief in her voice was evident.

"You have not heard how I will help you," Michael said raising his hand slightly to stem the flow of ideas. "Don't worry; I think you will be convinced." He assured Elizabeth. He had seen disappointment pass quickly across her face; this was a girl who was not used to hiding her emotions like the ladies in society usually did. The more Michael looked at her the more he was convinced she would enjoy herself with his help. "Stay in London for the Season."

"But I don't want to, and the estate in Yorkshire will be lost if I don't act fast." frustration was all too evident in Elizabeth's voice.

"I will secure the estate if it is, as you say, a suitable investment. If it is suffering from long term misuse, another year's neglect will not harm it any more than it has been already. I will have it assessed and see if there are any interim measures which may need to be put in place. In the meantime, you will stay with my sister as we had planned when I became aware of your existence. We will introduce you into Society, and you can enjoy the entertainments of the season. I understand your reluctance, but that should not stop you enjoying yourself at least once in London. You will be under no pressure from me to find a husband. If you find one, all well and good, and if you don't, at the end of the season you can retire to Yorkshire and have fond memories of your time here."

Elizabeth looked as if she was going to challenge him at first and met his gaze. She seemed to go from a challenge to a question and then shrugged her shoulders slightly and nodded. "As long as I can be involved in the buying of the estate, and I have your word that I can go to Yorkshire eventually, I will agree to stay in London for the Season."

"Good. Mr Hammond will take care of all the legalities of the Yorkshire estate as necessary. I will have my own estate manager, Charles Anderton travel there and look the place over. Don't worry; you will have the opportunity of speaking to him." Michael interrupted her before she could argue. "Now if you are not too tired, I would like to take you to meet my sister."

Printed in Great Britain
by Amazon